His Hope Her Wolf

Tanya Coleby

Published by Tanya Coleby, 2023.

This is a work of fiction. Similarities to real people, places, or events are entirely coincidental.

HIS HOPE HER WOLF

First edition. February 11, 2023.

Copyright © 2023 Tanya Coleby.

ISBN: 979-8215459829

Written by Tanya Coleby.

Also by Tanya Coleby

His Invisible Hold
Ruby Red - Ruby Dead

The Fable Gems
FLASHBACKS
Abduction

The human sensor series.
The Human Sensor
The Human Sensor 2

The Royal Dragon Series
The Dragon Flame

Vampire realm
His Invisible Hold
His Invisible Hate

Standalone
His Hope Her Wolf

To those that like the unknown.

As Clay does- have Hope.

<u>HIS HOPE, HER WOLF</u>
BY TANYA COLEBY
<u>NOW</u>

As Hope writhed around in agony on the floor of the forest of the camp that they had set up earlier, sweating profusely, Clay held her hand sweetly acting and cupped her face worriedly in a tight and protective firm grip and he lovingly wiped the sweat away from her worried face with a damp cloth. He had made it moist for her, from the flowing river nearby them.

She was burning up and nothing could break her fever.

Her golden-brown skin the succulent colour of caramel, was beginning to glow on and off in a rather strange way, which looked unnaturally freakish with its eerie shine.

She did not know what on earth was happening to her or why so? She wondered again why oh why, had she made the stupid mistake to come to this planet with Clay for a time? She was scolding herself now that she should have taken her time and not gone and made such a rash decision to go to there with him. And that maybe, just maybe she should have stayed behind on hers with the safety of her own people.

And those that were like her.

Her bones felt like they were snapping at all angles, and her joints burnt like a raging fire was running itself through them, and she felt like she was being burnt alive from the inside out.

"Clay what is going on here?" Hope said to her handsome companion on their trip for answers, with tears glistening in her usually brown eyes, which disturbingly to look at now had changed to a bright and vivid shining gold yellow, which reminded him of two blazing hot suns during sunrise. They were going from their usual shade of startling brown to a vivid bright yellow, and back again, with increasing consistency like they could not make their mind up what shade they wanted to actually so be!

But she looked simply beautiful to him either way, no matter what she looked like. She could wear rags and he would be on his knees begging for her to be his girl.

Clay the wolf shifter prince sighed quietly in his hidden anguish at her obvious excruciating pain, that he so desperately wished more than anything else in the world that he could take away from her weary body. And put it Into his own one. He would do anything for her, but he feared this was one thing that he could not overcome for her.

He turned to face Hope looking rather guilty like a young boy caught nicking sweets from a sweetshop and feeling it beyond anything also.

He did not know how to say it.

"I think I know what is happening here. But I am not entirely sure of it." He uttered.

But if it was what he thought, then it shouldn`t even be happening at all to her. It couldn't be! Not to his precious fated mate, she was nothing but a good person as ever. She didn't deserve this whole entire, painful transformation that he suspected was happening to her right before his very eyes, and which would be therefore permanent, and keep her from ever returning to her own world.

She begged him, her long eye lashed eyes looking into his own. Her gaze pinned him to his like she was a magnet.

"Tell me Clay. Please. I need to know. I need to know what is happening to me." She insisted that he tell her, no she begged of it. She didn't like the not knowing what was going on right now, even if the answer she got was one that she didn't want to hear right now.

He decided to just say it. "I think your.... I think your turning into a wolf like me, sweetheart."

Like him. But no, not the same as. For if it were true what was transpiring, for not a black wolf like him she would be. No.

But a golden one. The first of its kind ever to be in existence on his planet, and also the last one.

The golden wolf was said to be the one who would be fated to be the one to rule over them all. And to knock the current leaders off of their perch. The one from the prophecy that would bring them all together, and who would enable anyone to be able to find their fated mate from the age of eighteen onwards, and to sharpen their senses, to be able to find their other half at ease, and without any delay.

Not like now, where you only found your mate if they were in the same town or the same area as you, and you happened to lucky go and cross paths with them. It was rare unfortunately to find the other half of your soul. So, a lot of the wolves picked their own mates, even if they were not fated to be together.

For it was better to have a chosen mate then none at all.

You could also if the prophecy turned out to be true, scent them out from far away, giving everyone an equal and fair chance at fated mate hood, just like Clay had been lucky to have.

This had never happened before where an adult Triumphian from his home planet, had changed into a beast also, it had only happened to young wolves, cubs. But she was not from the planet Triumph, she was from elsewhere entirely.

From another planet far away from his. Too far.

With their species of wolf shifters, you got given your wolf, and it unleashed from your body at around six to eight years old, never just randomly at the age of twenty-six years old, like poor Hope was at the present time. Who had no wolf magic running through her blood, like everyone else on the planet nearly did.

"What!" What the heck! She looked at him both scared and also extremely horrified in one sweep. This couldn't be happening to her, it just couldn`t....

So, she decided to stay in denial, the best place to be right now.

She tilted her aching neck. "I`m not getting a wolf, your wrong that`s stupid! I think I`m dying Clay. That must be it. This must be the end, I can't bare it, I really can`t it hurts so bad." She sobbed openly and screamed out loudly her yell piercing through the land, as a sharp pain like nothing else, ran through her abdomen like she was being repeatedly stabbed in the stomach with a set of sharp knives.

"Or maybe I`m having a surprise baby?" She said as another cramp like what she knew of a contraction hit her stomach. She didn't think that she was able to carry a child, but theses thing could be wrong, couldn't they?

Clay openly growled out at that awful thought. The thought of her carrying a child that wasn't even his, and she looked up tear stricken and frowned at his reaction as she didn't know the extent of his feelings for her right at that moment, and why he growled aloud like he was beyond mad.

She argued with herself.

"But I haven`t you know...haven`t done the deed in ages except with you of recent. It has been more than nine months since another has gone there so.... Argh! What is this hell coming over me? What have I done to deserve this fresh hell?"

She didn't realise that her words were making the ever in control wolf want to unleash its anger to the world! He did not relish the thought that she had taken another man`s cock before his, even though he had no rights to her back before.

She didn't frankly care or wonder now why Clay was growing increasingly more agitated and struggling to reign his beast in. She was in too much pain to care.

But as it turned out though, Clay was sadly right. She was actually becoming a wolf. Right then. Right now. With haste.

For as soon as she started accepting and believing that it was happening, it and rather than denying it, golden light brown fur, started breaking out over her golden skinned, toned arms, and her white teeth seemed to be growing suddenly much longer, and extremely sharpened into points like they were fangs.

She disturbingly to her horror, let out an inhuman growl from her petite collared throat, and gasped in surprise at the unfamiliar sound being released from her own mouth. She howled, she actually howled!

She could not believe it!

"I`m.... I`m turning into a wolf!" This was not happening to her, she thought before she passed out from the pain. It had become too much for her. Her body was changing, and there was nothing she or anyone could do about it!

THEN

CHAPTER ONE

<u>THE JOURNEY TO TRIUMPH.</u>

Hope and Clay, who were two close, but fairly new friends were sitting closely and uncomfortably cramped together, like sardines in a can on their way back to Clay`s warm welcoming planet - the planet of Triumph finally. He was eager to get home to his people.

They were currently travelling to his home together in a magnificent but awkwardly small and compact spaceship, which Hope joked was the smallest one ever. It was brilliantly way faster than the speed of light, which was also causing some difficulty for them both, as it was located on the other side of their galaxy!

It was a bit of a bummer to get to by any means.

And it was one that was also on a completely different galaxy to the planet Earth!

Clay, apparently according to him and what he had told Hope since they had met, not that long ago merely a few months ago, gradually over their short time together on her world during friendly but cosy evenings hanging out together, lived on a beautiful, hot and tropical like, small planet filled with glorious stunning but dangerous water falls, wide stretches of rain forests and stunning warm beaches, with clear turquoise water to dip your toes in and relax for a while, and clean beige sands for the antsy, energetic wolf packs that lived there to pace along the shore.

Packs that happily graced the planet to run for miles across the flowing and ebbing waves, to stretch their furry, strong legs and to bond more with their rightfully chosen pack. The pack that they were brought up with from birth and who they would stay with until they so died.

The place where the group of shifters became at one with each other! Friends and family united together and merged until their days were done and their time on the planet was finally numbered.

Running behind and alongside, guarding their beloved king and queen of the shifters, who was also of course- their only Alpha and Luna. They would protect them at all costs and no matter what. They would even die for them. It was enabled by nearly all of the packs to protect the royals, and of course each other especially the young pubs and the old wolfs, except for the ones that pulled away from them all, that nobody liked to talk about...

-The rogues.

These were the shifters who were best avoided at all costs, unless you had a death wish. They didn't follow no rules, and therefore didn't care about their actions.

For there were many, many packs on the planet Triumph. Some blessed with their own chief who was royally appointed to keep things ticking over in the packs nicely, and to keep all rightfully in order. But they all answered to their king and queen who were also their Alpha and Luna, they were the top dogs- well wolves.

Some groups or single wolves of rouges ran things their own way though, and they couldn't under any circumstances no matter how hard the royals tried, be pinned down by rules. These were known as rogues, as they wouldn`t bow down to the ways or the abided rules of the planet, and there was every now and again a bid to try to take over the peace, which inhabited most of the friendly planets people.

A mutiny.

Because the gorgeous warm planet that Clay lived on, which apart from a few other species of different animals loitering around was also made up nearly entirely of big and black, all powerful and mighty wolf shifters!

She hadn`t believed it at first when he had first told her this piece of information.

It seemed to Hope like just mere fantasy on his part! He looked human, didn't he! Except he wasn't human at all...

Until that was, she had seen his inner beast ripping itself out of his body before she could even blink, with her own eyes that was....

This would be interesting Hope thought, as they seemingly at last neared their final destination, and she felt twanging waves of both excitement at seeing these people that he knew and loved as their wolves, and also in their other form as just mere normalish people.

Whilst also feeling a teeny bit on edge at what was to come in the not-too-distant future for her and for Clay!

Things were she admitted kinda complicated there. She liked him in the romantic sense, but she wasn't truly sure what he felt. Sure, he liked her he showed her it every day, but was it only as a friend thing? And that was not forgetting the whole mate thing that he had potentially going on, which she guessed didn't include her as his other half...

Maybe she wondered although it was probably more than a bit late now to wonder and have any doubts now if she had made the right choice in tagging along, now that they were nearly there at his home planet. And she pondered again If she should have stayed on her own world with her own kind of people, and all that she was used to?

But then where would be the fun in that!?

And besides, she definitely wasn't ready to let this hot and fiery one Clay, beside her with his gorgeous, delicious dark skin, big thick like tree trunks leg and arm muscles and firm abs, go just yet... And besides she loved an adventure which definitely hadn't happened much at her home due to the circumstances of her and her people, and the aliens that had regrettably invaded her home.

Yes, that is right- real life aliens!

And they had been scary as hell beyond measure. The stuff of your worst nightmares and far more than that.

And these ones didn't come in peace welcoming all and sundry to be firm friends for all of time with them and be allies forever more. No. They came to other planets and entered people's homes without invite, with only overwhelming hate and total destruction in their minds, on both Hope`s planet and also on Clay`s planet too.

Oh, and Clay who was sitting bunched up beside her, with the warmth of his hot animalistic breath in her ear, was also the one and only hot and dishy prince of all the wolf shifters on the planet. And he was also soon to be also the ruler and king and of course the Alpha as his dear, old dad was reluctantly due to his increasing age and dwindling health, handing over the reins soon to him to rule over everyone.

And everything.

His sister Shelly Ann was really the rightful future queen of them all by rights, but she was adamant and had been since she had grown up and finally became a woman, that she didn't want the drama of being in charge of it all. Shelly said that it made her panic, with alarm loudly ringing deeply inside. She didn't want to be the wolf queen of them all. Ever. So, she had happily handed over the next rights to rule to her baby brother. Clay. And she had had no regrets.

Their sibling relationship was as ever rock solid, and he had supported her as always, and had told her that the decision was only hers, and hers alone to make. Of course, he wanted to be king. Who wouldn`t? But it was up to Shell what she decided to do, and if she had wanted to be the queen when his parents passed the baton and be the Luna also, then he would have backed off and supported her decision, and he would have felt no resentment at it.

When he became the king and Alpha, he would cherish it and make them all proud of him, when the time came for him to rule over them all.

He, Shell said would be what they all so desperately needed for their future to play out in the way that it was intended, and she knew she really did, as she could sense certain things that one shouldn`t be able to sense so normally. She had known from the off that Hope would be special too at first contact with her back then, and she had gravitated towards one of her male friends in a way also that he had never seen her ever look at a male before. Like he meant something to her.

Something special.

Because she knew something that nobody else did. She was in tune with it all like no one but could be.

> Hope beside him was elsewhere in her head, away with her head in the clouds wondering inside secretly once like before when she had found out who and what Clay was which was a shifter as she could not voice it out loud, who would eventually end up as his precious, beloved wolf queen and Luna… Whoever they were, then she thought that they would be one lucky person- well wolf, to go and land that hunk of stuff as their forever mate that was for sure!

Cos just look at him!

He was simply divine! Magnificent! They had both kept themselves to themselves on her planet they had had to, but she bet on his home world that he would be fawned over by the eligible ladies and possible, and the eligible males too! And he wasn't just extremely good looking with a pantie twitching thick and sexy voice, that made you melt like butter. No. He was also fierce and courageous, and a good father now single father, to his boy at that.

He was like all her dreams put together plus more so.

A small pang of unexpected jealousy hit her stomach making her clutch it with her hands, which she tried to shake off and right herself. For she knew that she couldn't be jealous as she had known all along that things would have to be this way.

For he wasn't hers to have, was he? For she couldn't stake a claim to someone who could end up one day belonging to another female. It would kill her slowly from the inside out! No, in her mind it was better to keep her distance from him in the romantic way even though there was an extreme throbbing connection growing between them, and she had to keep her heart from becoming irreparable and broken by him.

She had had the pleasure of only seeing his wolf running free from his body it was truly magnificent, and it had hunting for the meat that it enjoyed, from afar in the night when safest to be, hidden in the shadows away from her peoples careful watch.

Because they couldn`t have found out what the shifters really were as it would have been dangerous for everyone involved for them to discover their true identity's. They would all have been put at risk if they had been discovered as wolves and as also aliens from another planet. It was a risk that they just couldn't take.

But when he had run with his young son and sister, and she had been there to witness he had been simply a magnificent creature!

She just couldn't believe she was in lust possibly love with a wolf shifter and not just one of a story tale either, but a real-life beast! It felt like a dream it really did.

He on the seat of the spaceship next to her, could feel her inquisitive gaze burning into him like an out of control fire at his large well-formed muscle y back, and so he abruptly stopped what he was doing which was looking out of the spaceship windows observing the movements from outside, at the whole entire magnificent and wondrous view of outer space around them, and instead turned to look at her.

He looked at her head on, gazing into her brown enticing eyes with his own startling pale-yellow ones, which glowed with his strong ever-changing emotions.

He was feeling it right now. His eyes were changing at the female who he adored so much sat there like an endless dream beside him, and on thinking of his return home where he so belonged. The home that he thought that he would never get to see again.

For her planet was OK, sure it was, and it was very different and made a nice but only temporary change. But compared to his planets temperature it was a cool place all over, and not nowhere near as warm as his own one was. He liked the fiery heat on his skin, and it was what his inner beast was used to. It also wasn't as developed there or rich as his home was.

The planets people regrettably seemed to be in a constant state of struggle all the time for things that they needed on an everyday basis, and the leaders in charge were tough on those below them and not helping things along either.

On his planet those in charge helped in any way that they possibly could. It was their duty too and the planet was more developed and had more potential then sadly Hope`s planet ever would do.

He turned his neck around to where his heart truly lay and stared at her for a moment lost in her eyes gaze, and he reached over and daringly to her secret and utter joy, squeezed her tanned, toned arm with a large soothing hand in reassurance of her evident worry. He smiled at her broadly, his smile lighting his stunning eyes in his happiness.

Causing her to feel all fluttery and giddy like a blossoming teenager from his stare inside herself, and nearly exploding from his gentle manly touch.

For this man was perfection to her!

This male that she was only just getting to know and hopefully would get to know more plenty, did strange and funny things to her inside that she couldn't explain away!

He was so protective of her, and she absolutely loved it.

Even if he was annoyingly hogging all of the room on the squashed and heavily compact seats, that Hope decided some Moron somewhere out there must have invented. Considering the fact that it was rather squashed for her nestled on them, and she wasn't even the biggest of people. So, she could only begin to imagine how he felt being confined in these small seats, with his big, thick, black muscley, handsome self-wedged into them!

He didn't complain though at any point on the trip about being squashed in though. And neither did his faithful men who had with everything that they could muster, bravely rescued them both. And who had been nothing but patient and polite to her since the journey began.

Who were admittedly not as well built as Clay no, but they were still like a group of amateur wrestlers with their thick set builds and endless muscles straining out of their too tight clothing, like it would rip their tops if they even dared to move the wrong way!

Their tailor must have a job and a half!

She decided that she wouldn't want to mess with any of them if she could help it, well maybe Clay, but then that would be more then play fighting with no clothes on if she had her way about it...She wondered if he would let her win a fight. She doubted it, he didn't seem the type to, and she could only imagine how dominant the man beside her was in the bedroom, like he was so out of it...

But she definitely wasn't complaining though at the way things had turned out in the end with their journey so far.

For although she wasn't sure how she felt for him at present right now as too much was occurring to set her thoughts straight, and it was making her head spin on the ins and out of everything. Or whether to act on it just yet as she wasn't quite ready for any romance with any suitor after her recent ordeals, and the troublesome events that had frightfully occurred for her back home.

She had been through a complete and utterly devastating ordeal when the blue, and dangerous psychopathic aliens the Hazguard`s had invaded her precious homeland. They had caused her all sorts of issues in her life that you couldn't ever manage to dream up and it would take a long time to fix things.

It was a knock-on effect, and It was still too raw for her to talk about for too long as it caused terrible feelings to build up inside her. Not that long ago after he had first laid his gorgeous twinkling wolf yellow eyes on her, then one of her closest friends who she had grown up with all her life from small children to now at the age of 26, had unexpectedly been brutally attacked when out for a romantic stroll with her new beau, also their closest friend, and had unfortunately to all their everlasting sadness, passed on to a better place. The death plain.

She missed her friend so very much; it ate away at her inside to know that she would never see Maya ever again! The grief was agonising and like nothing that nobody could explain unless they had been there themselves.

Alas she hadn`t been only the life taken by the aliens either, as the blue beings didn't care who they butchered or killed at all. As long as they got whatever they desired from their unsuspecting victims then that was the end of it. The blue and brutal beasts had wanted workers to do their bidding, and they wanted females for mating or disturbingly- for potential cross breeding.

Many had been destroyed by them in more ways than one. Physically, mentally and unfortunately in a few cases too sickening to comprehend -sexually too. Hope was relieved that she had managed to avoid being taken by one of those beasts into their lair on an island on her home planet. It didn't bear thinking about, it really didn`t.

Clay did not like seeing his Hope sitting there with her head in the clouds- Well in space, looking overly worried and in her silent distress which blared out in silent alarm which he could feel but not so see. For to him it was now his job to do the worrying for her, to shoulder her everyday fears, to be the man or wolf that she could lean on, and to rely on forever more.

Until death.

"Don`t be nervous my little Hope. Everything will be all-right. I give you my word so." He drawled at her in his sexy, thick accent that made her shiver inside with its unspoken promise, and to feel strangely at ease, and her tummy fluttered with her overwhelming longing, need and ache for him in her heart and also in her secret area. He completed her.

He felt the same way but more though she wasn't aware of it.

His soul called for her like it was a melody, and it dragged her straight into his own one with a long winding invisible string, that she did not know it would be forever entwined.

He spoke aloud from the silence except for the light humming of the ships engine.

"You will be treated well by my people I promise you Hope. I will make vastly sure of it forever more, so do not worry about that. For you have no need And if they do not treat you in the way that you should be treated, then they will once I have, shown them who wears the crown... Me." He smirked and his eyes twinkled very naughtily. His eyes crinkling in his amusement at his spoken words.

He as Simba said, couldn't wait to be king. He was fucking born for it!

He drawled at her confidently in his voice with his thick sexy accent that could if he chose, bring even the stiffest of women to her knees for him in her complete submission to him, and obeying his every want and needs.

But he did not want another for himself, for there was now only woman for him, and now there would always only ever be one.

If anything happened to her then god forbid it, he and his wolf would most likely become a pining empty shell grieving for life, for its precious lost only mate. For that was what happened when a wolf lost his bounded one.

She tilted her head expectantly, her thick and jet-black beaded hair swaying whenever so she moved. She smiled at him with her exquisite face and perfect teeth and rested her head and tried to get it comfortable on his thickly built, strong manly shoulder. He was so comfy to lay against like a plump pillow! And he smelt sooo good.

To her he didn't smell like a wolf should, which she imagined to be was like a doggy, wet smell, but instead his scent drew her in with a deep intoxicating smell that brought her to him in an unnerving and strange way. Which for some reason she couldn't explain away. It was the best thing that she had ever in her life smelt, and she could never get enough of his intoxicating scent in her nose.

She could taste it with her tongue making her mouth water with her unashamed desire for him. She missed it greatly like she was missing a limb when they were ever apart, which was not often thank goodness.

Which to be fair was not that often as since they had met then he had made it his mission to stay protectively by her side where he felt he belonged.

She was beginning to feel rather nervous as they nearer his world As not long ago a few mere months back, then she hadn`t even known that shifters even existed at all and if someone had said they did she would have looked at them and laughed out loud at the absurdly of it!

That was until one cool spring day, Clay`s young and adorable six-year-old son Ruddy who had been at the house hiding, cold, worn out, scared and hungry had knocked on the door asking for her households help, he had escaped from great danger and his family at the time were still firmly in it. Of course, she obliged. Who wouldn`t? No one would ignore a kid like that who needed her help.

Her and Clay had met a few months back, after him and his sister and his only son had been brutally torn against their will from their home planet by vile, uncaring savage, ugly beasts, and took to another one not that far away from there which wasn't even the aliens own.

It had been Hopes planet luckily for them both. Else they wouldn`t of even met!

His son Ruddy had thankfully much to their relief, managed to escape from the prison compound that they were all being held in, with also a variety of different imprisoned species all being held. He had managed to escape after his first shift ever into his wolf went wrong and he had become stuck. Stuck as half wolf and as half Triumph.

He had looked deformed like a mutant.

And he had managed to break out and find his way out of there, the island where the prisoners were held to find help and had ended up at Hope`s friend's house, where her and her friends were all in hiding from the violent species too - that were frighteningly trying to take over them all.

Not long after young Ruddy had reached there, then he was joined by his father and aunt who had thankfully at last managed to escape too after many months being held by the blue beasts.

But his mum was missing, presumed dead...

His young son had known then but he didn't know why that this female Hope, who had lovingly helped him in his great time of need. The female with the golden caramel skin lighter than his own, and black hair like his and friendly smile, for he would be ever grateful for would have a special place in all their lives.

Little Ruddy on his escape from the prison island had passed many homes on his journey from hell, but he had gravitated to where Hope was.

Why? It was a question that they all wondered in their minds but they hadn`t voiced aloud

Those blue beasts that took them all and stuffed them in their also small alien ship like sardines in a tin, were a brutal species of aliens who was run by a vicious, and evil queen. The beasts were out to dominate everything and enslave them all. And to work their way through the planets, and then through the Galaxy`s one by one and gradually taking over them all with their long, lanky, blue strange selves that couldn't even speak English, so most their prisoners hadn`t understood them.

Hope looked over to Clay`s sweet and adorable son who had joined them on the journey to back home. He had been jumping up and down with his young excitement when the ship arrived overhead in the skies on a rescue mission, finally at long last for them. Making dark fur disappear and reappear on his then too lean arms, and his small youthful eyes shine out like moons, a pale yellow.

Ruddy was still a young and new shifter and was only now learning to control his wolf. Which would take him time and much patience before his wolf settled down and he had control of it.

Also taking into consideration that his son had experienced something that no one, especially not a young one should ever have to go through which was to witness his beloved mother who was his dads best friend from childhood but not his mate but someone who he had been put with to continue their blood line, was cruelly and disturbingly attacked presumed murdered, right in front of his young eyes, and so his emotions were rightly all over the place. As anyone would be.

Little Ruddy couldn't keep his young wolf hidden and at bay in front of non-shifters, and therefore he had had to be kept inside most of the time in the day back on Hope`s world so as not to draw people to the fact that the three of them- he, his aunt and father were not from the planet at all, and were actually a trio of wolves, alien wolves! And also wolf royalty at that! If Ruddy had morphed into his wolf in the small-town centre, then it would have Majorly caused chaos and mayhem on the streets! Her people were already wary of outsiders after the blue beasts landed without being greeted by wolves.

The group had finally to their up-most relief been recovered from a small, quick and compact ship which had been sent from his base as the planet they were rescued from did not have spaceships on, or the knowledge to know how to fly to another Galaxy!

If they hadn`t been rescued by his people, then they would have been frankly rather screwed! They were all starting to think after all that time waiting for rescue and after many days had flown by, that that help was never coming to them. They had been on her world roughly six long and lonely months.

"That`s it my Hope." Clay said smoothly to her with his silky sexy voice in her ear like a lullaby lulling her to sleep with its eternal comfort, as she sleepily leant her petite head onto his shoulder now, and she started to doze lightly onto him. She was too worn out to care if she dribbled everywhere all over him! She just wished that these darn seats reclined more so she could lay down flat and not sleep propped up!

When she was firmly asleep and therefore couldn't overhear him, he whispered gently into her curved ear, so that no one else nor she could hear his private thoughts.

"Sleep my lady, for in the morning we will soon be at my home. Not just my home, for it is now yours. It is where you forever belong. With me. And as my rightful queen. And if anyone dares to try to take you away from me...." He pulled away from her ear so as not to wake her and growled lightly at that thought of anyone trying such a thing, he would beyond pulverise them! He would rip them apart with his wolf teeth!

His wolf eyes shone out brightly in the dark of the room, trying to break through his control. But failing.

He couldn't wait to be back home though. He had missed it so very much. His big and extremely well developed and manly thick chest, lit up brightly inside with his excitement at being back with his pack after 8 months away from them all.

But it did not light up as brightly as the golden skinned female beauty with black beaded hair like a charm, who was currently sitting next to him, the one who he knew but hadn`t said was forever made him.

She enticed his big, black dominating wolf in to the deep, dark abyss of back and beyond with her sweet feminine scent smelling like bees nectar to his senses.

He knew deep inside that this woman who no, wasn't even from his own planet at all, was in fact one of the rare legends that had only blessed a few of his kind. For she did not know it, but she in fact was-his fated mate. His souls destined one. Bound by the moon, they were two halves of a whole. He was blessed in every way now, and now that he had her next to him, he would forever be more now.

And she would whether she submitted by choice or not, eventually in time and when things were right- be his queen. The queen of all the wolves. Of the whole planet...

The next morning after a sweet and uninterrupted and deep slumber next to each other which was quite amazing considering how uncomfortable the seats actually were, the two close friends and his beloved and only child at long last reached his planet in due time.

They had reached it earlier than expected in fact!

It had taken them two long weeks, but at last they were there! At long last.

"Hopey, wake up." Clay grinned at her on seeing the planet appear before them in the ships large windows, and he lovingly caressed her lean shoulder gently with a large hand.

"We are here." He said. In awe.

"Already! I can`t believe it!" She tiredly turned and smiled happily at him, at the happiness that was on his handsome sculpted face at being back with his people, it was contagious to see. His smile made his handsome face even more handsome.

"Yes, we slept for over eight hours." Though it sadly seemed like mere minutes, and he was surprised after whispering in her ear that he had nodded off soundly mere minutes later. She soothed his soul, that she did.

"Wow!" She said surprised at that info but wishing secretly that she could sleep more.

She felt even more wow when she observed the planet shining bright and beautiful, in their near view as they approached it at great speed. Beautiful. It was just beautiful, beyond words. She wished that she had a camera to capture the beauty of it shining there in the depths of space. They were now starting to reach the planet and would soon get ready to land. She would miss her own one that she knew and loved, but she would try her up most to learn to love this one for the short or long time that she was on there.

For Clay.

"Clay?" She whispered quietly in his ear so that no one else could hear what words would leave her full lips.

"Yes, my princess." He said boldly, watching her full lipped face for her reaction at being called that particular pet name by him. Which she kind of was but didn't so know it. She blushed awkwardly.

"Oh, ha ha very funny. Your princess is out there somewhere Clay for you, don't worry you will find her I`m sure. Anyway. Clay.... I`m truth be told, a bit scared now that we are about here..."

The usually brave and bold heroic woman that he professed to know, confessed to the hulky man next to her who was silently waiting for orders to remove their belts, rise and prepare to depart the ship now that they were approaching landing.

He tried to hide his disappointment at her reply that she wasn't his princess that had made his heart skipped a beat, and answered her swiftly so that she wasn't aware of how her harsh words had bit through him like a thousand needles

"Why are you scared my beauty? And of what?" He asked his one. He was not often scared but he had been of late.

She laughed merrily at that remark.

"Beauty! Are you joking? I look like complete shat, and you well know it. Because Clay as you said, apart from the animals that run loose around this planet, or who are kept as simple house pets by your people, then I am the only non-wolf shifter person on the whole entire planet! The whole planet!" She gasped with increasing anxiety threatening to overwhelm her in droves. Her stomach had butterflies, and the butterflies also had butterflies.

"And?" He enquired.

As an all-powerful prince he was used to major upheaval in his, his packs and also his family's life on a regular ever occurring basis and of ongoing continuing problems, and her worry to him was nothing major that couldn't be solved.

"And?"

"They are my people my Hope, I am soon to be entirely in charge of them all and their one and one leader the king and wolf Alpha. So therefore, all of them, they will do exactly as I say, or they will deal with my fiery wrath and trust me when I say that you wouldn`t like to see me when I am angry. You really wouldn`t. It is not a pretty thing at all to have to witness."

He looked round at her and sighed, his eyes glistening and brightened to a bold shade of yellow then faded back to the usual pale yellow, and he touched her face boldly with a large dark thick fingered hand. He caressed it with his, making her gasp softly at his enchanting touch.

He was trying to keep his wolf inside himself with difficult ease at on touching her.

Hope asked him. "Why would I make you angry? I would do nothing to hurt or upset you, Clay. Ever, I promise you. I`m not bad." And she meant every word that she said.

"You wouldn`t." He dropped his hand angry that she thought that she could ever do that to him. Never! He let out an angry sigh at her not getting his explanation.

He turned and then blushed as her scent changed to something sweet like Triumphian candy. For she didn`t know the effect that she had on him with her presence, not just his on his intelligent all-seeing strong mind, but his whole entire body. She made his thick and large cock throb with ease.

It was surprisingly turning him on at the talk off her upsetting him, of her being bad and of him having to tell her off what with being her authoritative figure on his planet, and of having to discipline her.

Then he imagined that he would have to take her away, somewhere quiet with just them for her punishment, for it would be his and his punishment alone to deal out, which would likely consist of a good, hard and swift spanking and an enjoyable pussy pleasing, quick fingering.

He could imagine them afterwards, her sweet pussy juices dripping off of his thick fingers and tasting them naughtily to shock her into silence with his lips! He bet that she tasted like heaven between her lean firm thighs. He drooled at the thought.

He would enjoy that when it happened beyond measurement.

He decided that he needed to snap out of it soon and to compose himself for his extremely large, erect and black cock was getting even larger in his tight slacks and they would be ready to leave the ship that flies soon.

He adjusted himself discreetly in his seat quickly without anyone seeing and tried to calm his growing erection.

He could hear someone approaching them from the back of the ships room.

"Sire, we are ready for departure." A tall older male walked over to them from the back of the ship and bowed his head respectably to his prince. Hope had seen that Clay seemed well respected by the few of his people that she had met so far, and she was honoured to soon meet his small yet close family and those closest to him soon.

Butterflies were beginning to form in her stomach. She just hoped that they liked her, it was important to her that he did!

"Splendid." Clay nodded respectably at the male known as Heets. Heets was a good warrior who he was proud to work beside. But he still watched him go anxiously, until the male was far away from what was his.

He held out his hand to help his son up who stood unusually shyly near him like a spare part as he hadn`t been with his pack either in a long while, and his wolf had not long surfaced, and he held out another one to help Hope up from where she sat.

She beamed at him.

He whispered in her ear and said something that she wasn't expecting and so no one else in earshot could hear.

"Do not be offended Hope, but in public and when those are in ear shot, you need to address me as sire, prince Clay. Something respectful to me. Many call me their future Alpha, but as you have no wolf inside then there`s no need be from you. Or if you call me by a casual name then the people may take offence at you, which we don't want to happen when they have just met you!" He chuckled but with his face expressions, he was obviously not laughing really.

He was to her shock and understanding, being deadly serious.

"Of course!" She stuttered lightly and frowned. She hadn`t thought of that, it was lucky that he had said that, or she might have offended someone that she didn't want to offend, like his parents! She had always since she had known him just used his name, as on her planet where they met, he wasn't a prince there, he had been just a mere wolf man.

She felt uncomfortable by what he had said but tried not to take offence. It was just his peoples way she supposed.

The tall, large and noble warriors on the spaceship, got out first so as to protect their boss and future alpha as it was protocol to check for danger first most, Clay made sure they kept their distance from her, why she did not know. Then they were followed by his adorable son who waltzed along happily with small excited happy steps, Clay with his large dominating confident steps, and then Hope after with more careful ones.

CHAPTER TWO

An older male and female who could only ever be Clay`s parents as they really shared a very strong resemblance to him both in looks and stature, and they were also surrounded by tall, strong and thick noble armed warriors armed to the hilt, who stood there waiting silently and patiently for them all to leave the ship at long last, with eager eyes.

His parents stood together clutching hands with happy tears building up in their welcoming eyes, on seeming them all slowly disembark from the compact spaceship and preparing to finally return to their home.

Where they should have been all along.

Many cheering and happy crowds of watching people, were beginning to gather around the ship, circling it and those people who had been busy out working the land that time, or in large impressive looking, decorative shops nearby, stopped whatever they were currently doing, and they quickly and without delay downed their various shaped assorted tools with a hasty clang, and shut their shops in a hurry to see what was going on, and to also see who was coming out of the ship.

Those that were not in eye of the ship came also, for news travelled fast and the princes return was like a game of Chinese whispers.

Those in the pack who were at that moment in their Wolf form respectively morphed back into to their normal person form, and they curiously came over to the ship as well, until it was just like a sea of people surrounding it in droves. They were obviously all rather excited, for at last their beloved lost and stolen wolf shifter prince, was now hopefully back home where he had been badly missed and was safe and well with his son and the others the guards, who had been so brutally, and unsuspectingly snatched and taken from their planet! And took to another!

That would be the main thing that they could take from that experience. That they were all safe, and they were back.

"Son!"

The powerfully built lady stood before them, but who was also very stunning for an older woman, rushed over as soon as she saw Clay`s rather large feet reaching the city land, which if he even was a smaller built bloke, would of almost certainly knocked him over from where he stood with her firm and heavy grip and running into him, on his contact with the firm, grassed ground!

She had a grip on her that was for sure!

"And my beloved grandson!" The well-defined thick and powerfully built dark female, turned her powerful body around and beamed at little Ruddy happily, her red lipped grin honest wide and long, as she lovingly picked up her beloved and only grandson in her strong, powerful arms, and swung him round and around merrily, and then when they stopped, she pretended to gnaw on him, to eat him to his squealing happy delight.

She obviously didn't care that she was the queen and needed to keep up appearances, for her adored family were now back, she wanted the world to know how much they meant to her!

"Nanny! I mean your majesty!" the spun boy giggled at her, feeling a bit sick by all the twisting and turning, so soon after their landing.

Ruddy said once she had set him down on the ground on his small feet, then bowing to the queen cheekily, and everyone chuckled at his young and childish sweet ever innocence. The lad then before them all, proudly flashed his pale-yellow eyes glowing ever so brightly, to show them all there in the pack, that he had finally gotten his wolf. Just like they had.

He was so proud of his wolfs first showing bless him.

"You actually got your own wolf!" His nan and queen said to him with a gasp, and she embarrassingly to her grandson sniffed him rather sharply with her long turned up nose, and immediately sensing his wolves inner beast hidden inside him at once, just there at the surface, with her sharp and keen senses. She was pleased as punch for him on him getting his beast she truly was, it was more than apparent, how much her grandson meant to her also.

"I can sense him. Well done young one!" The queen said honesty to the beaming boy. He beamed at her proudly and puffed his small chest out with his glee at her encouraging words.

For he was truly one of them now. A proper shifter for all of eternity. Wait till he showed his friends his wolf!

It was a truly big thing for the shifters wolf to develop at last inside their soul, and normally the child had a massive party in their honour, when their wolf had finally arisen from its hidden slumber, a party to welcome their wolf to the fold.

They would all then run together as a pack, with the newest member experiencing its first group run. It was a hell of a rush!

He had unfortunately not been there on the planet to celebrate it with all the others, at the time his wolf had first came out to play. Little Ruddy sighed in remembrance at his wolf coming at last to him, in the most brutal of ways, and at the most inconvenient time which caused him to be twisted and in pain, and on another planet at that....

It had been but a nightmare.

Their wolves was there from birth of course it was it was a part of them, and before then obviously. But the inner beast only materialised at the age of six to eight, whenever the young one was ready at last to receive it. To nurture it and be able to learn to control it.

When their wolf came to, then they could finally hear it in their mind, and communicate with it, and to also be able to hear their pack members inside their mind through their packs link. And the alphas orders of course when the shit hit the fan, and he needed their help with something or other.

Wolves didn't usually have fated mates, and if they did most sadly never discover them. As they could literally be anywhere on the planet, so only a handful was blessed with them or got the opportunity to meet them. Clay`s parents however were fated mates though, and it seemed much more common in royal pairings to find their other part.

Clay had always had a feeling in his bones since he had come of age that he would meet his one, the one made for him and only him, and his inner wolf as guided to him by the one and only moon goddess. But his fated one had never much to his agony, come to him when he became an adult at the age of eighteen like he had thought she would, and he had never found her, and he was now 30 so he had started to think that it would never happen....

And maybe he was mistaken?

Could you so wish for something to come true, that you lay awake in hope when you know that really there was none...

After five years of no mate, then his parents had finally put their foot down with their only son as you normally met your mate at 18 if you ever had the luck of doing so.

He had therefore been matched not by force but by very strong suggestion with his female best friend Charmain in the end. Which he had been thankful for, he wanted someone by his side to carry the burden of life, and to eventually rule by his side as his wolf shifter Luna and queen. Plus, he wanted little Clays of course!

Yes, the love he had felt for his child`s mother had been out of this world, but he and he assumed she, had never liked each other at all in the romantic sense like a mates should do with their partner.

And so, they both had agreed that if one of them ever had the pleasure and joy of finding their mate at long last, then the other one would release each other to them. After their son was born of course for his happiness was key as well.

And since their small wolf son was born six years ago then they hadn`t ever entered each other's bed chambers, but instead after one uncomfortable but truthful awkward discussion that involved a night of strong wine with each other and a disastrous try at love making, they had decided instead to take lovers.

But they decided that they must each be discrete, out of respect to the other one. For that was only fair.

Charmain had more than obviously preferred woman anyway he could tell from when her head turned when a beautiful looking female entered the room, instead of when a male so did. And it wasn't due to her of other females no. His friend was always as easy coming as they come and she hadn`t done jealousy. She wasn't like that!

One night upon returning to the place, he had seen a stunning and worn-out looking female leave her room, so he guessed that he had been right all along with his closest friends and picked mates, romantic tastes. He bore her no ill will though he never would, and he had agreed as he just wanted his best friend to be happy.

He himself had preferred someone that he actually had a romantic spark with as well and that wasn't Char unfortunately. she was like a sister to him; he had known her since they crawled around in nappies! The few times that they had made love with each other, had been beyond awkward for them both he wasn't ashamed to admit it!

He since then much to his building frustration had mainly used a firm hand many times each and every night, to find his firm and shuddering liquid release, and each morning on waking, so as not to complicate things with all the eager females that he knew wanted to be his mate instead of Char.

Because if he gave into some of the other females advances that clambered around, then they would want more from him. And more then he could possibly ever give them in return.

There had been only one lover for him which he regretted more than anything now for it had been an error of judgement, and now it would have to be knocked on the head now, that he had met his match. His Hope.

The Alpha and Luna looked behind him peering their strong necks round curiously and seemed to notice at once that his only sister was missing from the ship where she should have been- The Princess Shelly, his beloved older sister.

His mother quickly spoke up anxiously straight away. There was no dilly dallying for this particular woman!

"Where is your sister Clay, is she here? Is she well? Please say she is OK!" His mother started to more than panic now in front of her followers, her face paling gradually with her maternal unease and overwhelming worry, that something terrible had befallen one of her beloved children.

For it would kill her.

She had been definitely looking forward to seeing her beloved only daughter and first born again soon, and them being united and catching up as well as with her son. They were close knit.

Letting their wolves run together as a family. She had yearned for it since they had been taken, she wanted them all together. Family was certainly important to the shifters living on the planet of Triumph!

He knew that his next words that he spoke would really disappoint their mum somewhat, but she honestly deserved to know why his sister truthfully wasn't there from the compact ship. She was an adult after all there was no denying that, and Shell could do what she wanted much to their mothers dislike.

He tried to explain carefully and cautiously without further startling his mother the queen.

"She decided to stay there on the other planet mother, for a time. Don't worry, she will be back, you can't keep her away now I don't so imagine, she misses you both dreadfully! But she shall we say- has taken to one of the locals and he her, back on the other planet!" He laughed.

His sister had become taken to one of the male residents that Hope was close friends with there. A particular blonde and handsome male called Shane, with surfer dude good looks, and also thankfully -a heart of gold. A woman's wet dream, he supposed thinking jealously about the man near his Hope as he liked to be, they were friends after all.

Clay didn't realise that to everyone else that knew him, that he was a complete and utter hottie in his own right. Drool worthy. Many a female on the planet had wondered what lay beneath his under garments.

The queen grunted and rolled her yellow eyes.

"Oh, as long as she won't be away from us long! She must come back soon. We miss her so desperately. We all do!" His mother responded sounding like she felt let down by her daughter. Ut oh!

"I know you do mother." Clay sighed.

They had both greatly missed her it was obvious, and Shell missed them also, that was the bare truth and she had told Clay so herself with her own words. But she had things that she needed to work out with Shane before she returned home, so he had left her there for the time being. And she would be back where she belonged when she was ready to.

"The male that she is with. He`s an… an alien? One of those… Outworlders?" The queen spat out angrily, her eyes bulging as she spoke the words, she never expected to ever say out loud.

His normally pleasant kind mother spat the words out like it made her stomach rot from the inside out, and she looked really displeased at the entire idea of it all. Her daughter and a E.T, together! She shivered blatantly in her fear at the thought, of her precious but headstrong daughter even mating with an alien, barbaric, indeed! How embarrassing…

The hulky wolf prince tried to calm the queen down, but it seemed to be going in one ear and out of the other, which was typical for his dominant mother.

"Yes, she is, but she`s fine mother I promise, and trust me, he`s fine with Shelly Ann or else I would have dragged her back here with me when we left. And alone at that!"

He said to his mother curtly, and now trying to think of ways of how to change the subject, away from his beloved sister before his mother the queen exploded in a fit of rage, at not getting what she wanted!

Truth be told that the blonde alien male, Hopes best friend was a really big sore point to him. A complete pain in the butt.

But Clay did in fact only want the best for his beloved big sister like any good brother would, and for her to be as happy as she so rightfully deserved.

Which was a lot.

Clay had just been really glad that Shell had took the other males attention away from Hope's direction. But Hope had been adamant on multiple occasions though that the two of them- Shane and herself, were just very good friends, but Clays wolf and himself were so possessive and needy of her, they craved her, and much as she liked her precious friend who she had grown up with, they hadn't like another male hanging around her in return, and in her personal space all the time.

He tried to curb it in he really did, and to stop being so jealous but it couldn't be helped.

He wanted his mate happy at all times, and he also wanted to be the main reason that she was always happy. And if he had to put up with her annoying male friend hanging around them in their company like an unwanted bad smell, then so be it. And after one uncomfortable situation, Hope had told Clay off about his frosty behaviour to her friend making him uncomfortable, then after that he had tried to be pleasant as he so possibly could while he was there with him.

As much as he possibly could so anyway.

He was half wolf and a future alpha after all, and wolves were territorial creatures on a good day. A warning glint of his wolf shining bright eyes at the invading blonde male, when Hope wasn't looking was enough to make the male keep away from him so much! Secretly shaking in terror. Good! And since Hope had spent more time with Clay of late, then it kept him away from her too so much!

His parents the current and all great king and queen of all living on the planet, suddenly to Clay and Hopes relief, stopped their antsy fretting over their missing only daughter, and then they frowned and looked puzzled, at seeing Hope leaving the ships bridge now cautiously, looking at all those around and Clay with a scared face, like she was a deer stuck in headlights.

large and confused frowns appearing on the royals lined faces.

They was not pleased that was for sure.

"Who is this female? Where is our Char? Is she with Shell? Where is she!" His mother demanded of him, and then to her sons bemusement starting to get hysterical on seeing Hope walking down the bridge behind them all, and not in fact who it should have been which was his child`s mother.

Charmain. Missing presumed dead at that.

Charmain had been shot out of sight by ones of the blue alien beasts, out of sight behind an outbuilding. The alien had returned covered from head to toe in blood and guts dripping from its lanky body, so they assumed that she had sadly met her early end. They had heard the shot ring out, they had heard a loud thud. It had been a horrifying sight that was forever etched on Clay, Shelly and Ruddy`s brains.

He spoke quietly so that those people who were around the spaceship could not hear his next words, as it was not the time for them all to know what had happened to her, before her own family so did.

That would not be fair to them at all. They deserved to know the horror first.

"Your majesty, mother." He said.

"Something came up when we were held prisoner on the other planet with Char. I have some terribly bad news. She, I strongly believe, has passed on to a different plain. The death plain." He lowered his head in his sadness at the loss of his best friend in the whole wide world, and he was ever more hoping that his mother would get his silent meaning, and that she would not press him for more info on the subject.

Like she normally would.

He just couldn't go into details right now, it was still too harsh for him to even think about, let alone talk about. It was why he hadn`t in the end begrudged Hope and Shane`s close friendship as his and Chars, if she hadn`t have been brutally killed, would have been ongoing despite of Clay having have found his future wife. She would have been thrilled for them!

Clay warned them quietly.

"We will discuss it when the three of us are alone please, and we need to let her family know first of all before any others. Wherever she so is now, then she is at peace now. And she will forever be free from further sorrow, and pain. And I hope I always did right by her" He nodded at his parents and crossed his fingers over his chest in a respectful gesture to the departed.

His best friend.

"Son." his parents gasped and nodded at him back in their sudden understanding at what had obviously occurred during Clay`s forced imprisonment. Awful news, their poor son and grandson must be gutted they both thought! His mother sniffed and welled up sadly, and his dad gave her a reassuring pat on the arm and smiled at her gently. Her eternal mate.

Clay continued on warily in case his mother the queen went into further hysterics and drew further attention to them.

"Anyway. After all the bad, here we have the good." He drawled thickly his voice cutting through the air.

He gestured to his sweetheart.

"This is the rather lovely and sweet, Hope." He introduced her whilst he reached out a large hand to help her off the tilted down bridge. As it was slightly steep, and uneven in all the wrong places. And he couldn't so bear it if she fell down and hurt herself in anyway and did so because of him.

She took his warm palm gratefully with her own, enjoying his brief touch with her own.

It was all well and good for just a mere moment, but then as soon as her worn out feet actually left the ship`s bridge and touched the planets soil, then something unusual happened between them that was unexpected!

For as soon as she touched the land with a single foot, whilst also holding Clays possessive hand to help her down, then a weird and strange tingling and shocks went down each other's arms, causing them both to cry out in their shock and surprise, at the increasing shocking feeling running through them both in sync!

On her skins impact with Clay, her eyes went and changed colour, then back again, and his shone out brightly like crescent moons, and then dulled back to pale yellow like before.

You had to see it to believe it.

Much to Clays surprise, the fated mate bond was now kicking in with a jumping start. It was obvious.

It had to be that! It had obviously started for what he didn't know would happen, as soon as she reached where she was destined to be. Which was on his planet, and while she was there by his side.

Forever. As his future queen and the wolves true Luna.

He thought that they would both have had more time for all this. For her to recover mentally from her past troubles back on her home planet, and for him to become the next king first. And for them to do what needed to be done for his family and for his people, first most.

Then and only then would he be ready and her too, for them to become eternal mates. They had all the time in the world. Or so he had thought anyway.

"What was that!" Hope cried out quickly and letting go of his hand quickly, as so as not to hurt him. It had happened before, but not on touching him and it was a different sensation to before. She was proper stressing out over it! She couldn't bear to hurt him, she would rather never touch him again although that would hurt her deeply, then to inflict pain onto the alpha hunk stood there beside her.

"I`m not sure what it was." Clay blatantly lied to her face, and she was fully aware that he was, when he averted his gaze from hers, and looked guiltily at the soft ground around them.

Hope knew that he was lying. They all did. He wouldn`t meet her gaze as though he was hiding a truth from her. But why in god's name was he lying to her? She had thought that they were friends, and friends didn't keep things from each other....

Did they? No, they didn't.

"Is that?" his dad said finally speaking and looking amazed at what just happened between the pair, and butted in. Looking from Clay to Hope, and back again. He pushed forwards and towards his son with his thick, imposing royal figure, who was busy feeling flustered right then and trying not to stand too close to Hope, in case the tingling and shocks came back with a vengeance.

And gave him some more explaining to do.

His parents would know though without fail what was going on between the pair, what with being one of the only fated mates pairs that lived in their gorgeous city. They had been together like at least forty years, and they both knew each other inside and out! And they could see those that were a mated pair from anywhere.

And Clay and Hope was obviously one.

The shock on contact in the early stages of mates meeting, was a major give away to it!

"No." Clay said bluntly, and not meeting anyone`s eyes again with his own. He didn't want anyone to know yet what the truth was, just him. They wasn't ready to move forward like that and in that way, and it could put her in great danger from the rouges, if they found out that she was his mate. - From the pack less wolves. The wolves who didn't want one.

"Is what, what? Hope asked the shifters gathered around her, concerned at what they were keeping from her, as she knew that something was going down, but no one was letting her in on it. Feeling like an outsider already on the strange planet that she had just stepped on. Lovely.

"Another time. Now is not the time, Hopey." Clay ordered her in a calm manner and yet again backing away from her when she moved to close, as if she had the plague.

"Does this mean what I think it does my son? And I don't sense her wolf anywhere, is it blocked somehow from being sensed by any others?" His mother really stubbornly enough wasn't taking no for an answer, when he had said that they would talk about this another time to her...

The queen seemed to have strangely taken a firm and instant disliking, to Hope. Which was not what Clay would have expected from his mother at all.

"I.... I don't have a wolf." Hope said honestly to the planets only shifter queen. She wasn't a wolf, but gods be damned she wasn't going to be ashamed of herself because of it! She was still a person in her own right.

Clay saw his parents vacant expressions on hearing that Hope was wolf-less and decided to try his up most to diffuse the situation.

He spoke up.

"What she says is right. But it is irrelevant to me. As it should be for you. Come." He insisted to them all and gesturing towards the long, winding path and their home in the not too far distance. And so, they all took the small walk towards the large, looming and spectacular palace that they all currently dwelled in whilst the family who had missed their kin so much chatted small talk amongst each other, whilst Hope listened. Because at long last they were all together.

The magnificent and beautifully crafted palace before them was that humongous on seeing it, that Hope thought that it could probably fit the whole town comfortably in plus many more besides! Wowsers!

Hope was just amazed at its splendour and the moat that surrounded it and the draw bridge; it was like something out of a fairy tale!

Compared to her own mild planet, where she had spent her whole twenty-six years, then it was so hot here. It was like where she lived in the summer, but it seemed to be like that all the time! She could feel sweat beginning to form on her calm face and it was starting to seep under her arms, and it was then soon trickling down on her golden tanned skin.

She wiped it away. Phew. The weather was pleasant and made a nice change so it did, but it would take some getting used to for Hope.

She soon felt out of place as she looked and came from a different place, and her and Clay and his son were in very casual trousers and tops as the standard for many of her people were, whereas his people were all mainly in silky, smart garbs or pretty and flowing dresses and his parents were in glorious, sparkling jewelled outfits that glistened in the morning sun. The people here all seemed to like donning smart clothing, and they all appeared to be comfortably off, from what she could see so far at first sight.

The shifters were also all noticeably as well all black people, which was cool of course it was. But she was born of mixed race, and she had a lot paler skin tone to them. It shouldn`t matter obviously it shouldn`t, and it had never been an issue for her before then, as her and her friends back home were all different looking to each other. Her friend Shane was pale and blonde, Maya had been ginger with beautiful freckles, and last but not least Lynette had had brunette waves running down her back.

But anyway, the difference in looks between her and his people, were just slightly more noticeable here!

She would stand out from the others wherever she so went. Even if they didn't know her then they would notice that she was a stranger from another world, as she would stand out from the crowd. She as an out-worlder could be something that someone would be fascinated to see and to admire from afar, but she in front of the wrong person could also have a large target on her back or make them feel frightened of her as she too them- was an alien. Plus, she had no wolf!

She really was beginning to think that she hadn`t thought this whole visiting another planet thing through properly!

Luckily her hair was a gorgeous shade of vivid startling black like most of the rest of them, so at least they all had that it common with her!

She wondered why ever since the spark had literally happened between them, that Clay was keeping far away from her as if he felt afraid of her touch now.

And avoiding her touch. She wondered if it was her fault, that they had shocked each other? Was he angry at her? She didn't think so as he wasn't like that, she was sure from knowing him and his blunt ways so far, that he would say so if he was cross at her actions or words, as he usually did!

She did not know why it had even happened but thinking back she realised that it had happened as soon as her feet had touched the strange planets soiled ground. She was not used to him being so far away either, as since they had both met back then he had been there protectively by her side, as they had slowly built up quite a nice friendship, alongside playful flirting and teasing thrown into it.

She had over the past couple of months enjoyed spending lots of time with him and his son just the three of them, walking through her town together. Showing the place off to them. She knew that he wasn't hers to keep not really, but sometimes she just shut her eyes tightly shut, and then imagined the three of them as a family one day. Her as Clays forever mate, and as little Ruddy`s protector and step mum...

After an accident as a teen, she had ruined her chances of ever being able to carry her own child herself. Clay in fact, had been one of the only people that she had ever told the truth too. Ruddy wasn't a replacement child to her own no, never. She just loved him in his own right, whether her and his dad ever got together she would still no matter what came their way, be there for the growing lad always.

Their bond was strong.

When they finally crossed the long wooden drawbridge and reached the palace grounds, and walked through the massive security gates, Clay and his family went to deal with some vital business for the day. He turned to Hope and said that he would be over to see her later he promised that he would, and then he told her to make herself at home and settle into the palace, and to do whatever she wanted.

As she always could. Her happiness lit him up from the inside up.

She however when he had gone off to his boring meeting, wanted a nap and a freshen up and a helpful assistant showed her to where she was going to be staying for the foreseeable future.

Helpful but obviously curious that this person had no wolf inside.

Her room that she had been given to stay in was to Hopes disbelief, absolutely huge. It was even bigger than her whole cottage way back home! She had a quick wash, freshened herself up, then raided the larder fridge under the worktops for something good to eat, then went to the other side of the room to do her hair nice for Clay, as it by then was probably all over the show.

There was a large jewelled, decorated mirror on the wall that she admired the beauty of it. She looked in it whilst chewing the rest of her delicious freshly made bap, good like nothing she had ever tasted before it was delicious, and then screamed out loud at what she saw facing her there in the mirror.

For looking into the stunning mirror, she could see that her black, beaded hair that she had grown, was now a vivid shade of golden twinkling brown, glistening magically! She shook her head in disbelief and wiped her brown eyes, hoping to god that she was imagining things from their long and tiresome journey there.

She looked again, hoping that she was seeing things from being beyond shattered right then.

Nope, it was still a shade of golden brown! She couldn't wait for Clay to return so she could ask his opinion on her hair changing colour completely. She trusted him she so did. Even if he was acting shifty for some reason today, she still trusted the infuriating but devilishly handsome alien shifter male.

For was this planet changing her into something different? But if was so, then why?

Clay stood next to his parents the wolf shifter planet`s only king and queen. The only alpha and Luna on the planet as well. It was good to be back home on solid ground and familiar territory. He breathed the air deeply in, his planets rich air inhaling the warmth coursing through his huge, toned thick body, and enjoying the unique scent of his planet that he had missed so much in his long time away from it.

His dad the king and their alpha, narrowed his beady eyes at his son in knowing, as though he could read his deep and dark most inner thoughts that were circling his sons head. It was just the three of them now in the magnificent throne room as the others had left to give them all some much needed privacy. And Ruddy was in his room reuniting with his beloved toys that he hadn`t seen in ages, and he would be spending a few months in the castle to recuperate from his ordeal, and to learn to control his new wolf. So, they were finally free to talk in private without intrusion. Or so they hoped anyway, for some of their people could be nosy and wanted to know everything that was going on, and without any delay.

Clay wasn't fazed though.

He stood his magnificent, sculpted body proud and tall, with his arms carefully folded in front of his person, and bravely faced his parents head on. They were the king and queen yes of course they were, but he was also their son first most, and he would do things on his own term in his own way and fuck the consequences!

He wasn't no pushover! Soon he would have the throne. And he would take better care of it then they had.

"We never thought that you would return to us son." His father said with tears in his wrinkled slightly, lined eyes. He was a large and imposing figure too like his son was, maybe even bigger then him. He had thought that his only boy was dead, and that had hurt beyond anything that one could ever feel.

Clay had been taken by the aliens along with others, when trying to save his son and he had not come back for months. Eight months!

Their child was a man now, yes, he was. But he would always still be their little boy to them, the future alpha and king or not. They had been simply scared and terrified, when the aliens swooped down to their planet and stole Clay and his sister, and little Ruddy away. They thought with all the guards that they had in the city protecting them all, that they would all be safe from the dangers lurking deep in the forest, and from any out-of-control packs.

For yes, they did rule the whole planet, but not all of them were agreeable to it and its rules and ways. They would hold their own though, or they would all die trying to.

But while they were all looking around with watchful eyes and watching their backs for ever dangers that might be out there, then they hadn`t looked the most dangerous place of all- Up. For this is where the large, looming spaceship had come from.

"I am home now mother and father, and that is all that matters now." Clay said standing strong before them. But also, with them again. A family.

"But what of the female?" His mother piped in nosily. She was blatantly concerned about Hope and her intentions and reasoning for coming back with him, but it was only his business. And his alone.

"She is a.... a simple friend to me." He lied straight to his parents faces. He lied to them, and he lied to himself.

His father knew otherwise, as his own mate was beside him and he knew all the signs of an fated mate. Did Clay think that the king and queen were born yesterday?

"Your mate! She is your mate isn`t she Clay?" His dad said speaking up. And going over and making himself at home on his beloved throne that would soon one day be Clay`s, with a foot shuffle and pulling his heavy, decorated, jewelled robes to the side out of the way.

His mother just merely raised a lone eyebrow at her hard work son and obviously hoping that it wasn't true for she herself couldn't see it, or she didn't want to see it anyway. He knew how she would feel on the matter it was apparent, and it wouldn`t match his feelings at all he could tell. Only his ones mattered there anyway. And Hope`s.

"Yes." He paused deciding to be brave and to divulge the truth to those he loved, starting with his parents. They had always shown him great love and understanding.

He tried to explain. "But I am not ready to progress with things father at this point in time, and neither is she right now. We have both been through a lot these past few months together, while I was torn away from her father. Our bodies are fit and strong like fierce and noble warriors, but our minds are not at the moment. They are still weak, and they will need plenty of time to recover, before I overwhelm her that she is the future queen, and also the Luna of an entire planet. She is a good person and does not need to be pushed into anything right now"

He fidgeted on the spot at the thought of having to tell Hope all, and then sighed showing his discomfort at being put on the spot by his what he thought were, really interfering parents

"She is your mate?" An abrupt but shrilled female voice piped up, from behind the door in a simple question to those who stood in the room. Damn it! Clay was not at all happy, that someone had overheard what he had wanted to keep a secret from the people, for the time being!

Out strode confidently when they should be ashamed from the shadows, someone who had obviously been hanging around the door eavesdropping. There stood a female that Clay unfortunately knew all only too well.

The ear wigger was none other than the Beta, Davidson`s daughter-Star, a stunning, fearless woman, but who in Clays and most people's opinion was also a nasty, vindictive piece of work to boot. She had caused many dramas and rumours in her days, nearly caused rogues to attack with her careless spoken words, nearly causing a civil war, and she liked playing the males off against each other.

It was a sport to her, and she didn't care who got hurt along the way, as long as it was her that they were all fighting over, she didn't care.

But she only wanted one male. And that male was Clay!

In Clay`s eyes she wasn't bright and shining like what she was named after, no. But she in his opinion was dull and blunt.

She had had her beady, greedy eyes on him, wanting him for her own since they were both just pups growing up together, and there had been uproar from her and her family when Clay had been matched with Charmain and not with Star. His parents had given Clay the choice, and he had said that if he had to be in a loveless mate match, then it would only be with Charmain. And not Star.

So once Star went and found out his partner Char had been killed, then it would only increase her ever growing interest in him, and her eyes would be on the target tenth fold if she didn't know so of the news already.

"This is private business now Star, it is not for others ears." His mother scolded Star lightly.

She was close to his mother, and so he knew that she would let her off easily whereas others would have been punished for being dis respectful. She really needed for people to stop letting her get away with things, and when he was Alpha then he would put his foot down with her and her interfering dad. He would maybe even get a new beta!

For there was being nice to the people, and then there was letting people walk all over you and taking advantage of you, which is what Star and her family had done of late in Clays` view! He thought this quietly to himself.

And he knew that harsh as it was that his parents were too nice to be in charge for very much longer.

Before he got taken away things were slowly starting to unravel in the main city, and the rogues were starting to pop out of the shadows, more so then ever. When he ruled as the rightful king, then the rogues would join them all in the packs or they would be destroyed.

"I am sorry your majesty." Star said sullenly, her beautiful head down. "Luna, let me explain myself here please. I just passed the room that we are in, and I went and overheard what you were saying. I apologise. I am truly sorry." She lowered her head again in her fake submission to the royals with her, her yellow eyes slightly glinting out dangerously, and her lip curling smirk, obvious only to Clay who out of the three knew what she was truly like.

She truly wasn`t sorry for snooping, and Clay knew it. Not by a long shot. She didn't know the meaning of the word. He thought to himself that as if he would let a female like that lay in his bed every night, and to become the future queen, their Luna! She was way to selfish to rule as she only thought of herself

The problem for him was she had actually unfortunately already laid in his bed multiple times, and that is where he stupidly went and made his first mistake. By thinking with his eager and horny cock, and not with his head which is what he should have done.

But now that he knew what she was really like, as he had seen it for himself, and he had seen through her pretence then he would not repeat the same mistake again. And he would have to keep her away from Hope, for she could not be trusted to behave.

For she was a beauty no one could ever deny it. And she could fuck well for sure, but she did not have a pleasant personality or any care in her dark heart, or enough honour for him to trust her beyond that!

She turned to face Clay now and gave him a flirtatious leer, then a wink.

"So, Charmain has passed on, and you now conveniently now she has gone have met your fated mate? Even though fated mates are as rare as they come here. And one that is not a wolf but a ...but a nothing by the smell of it. And she`s also not black like the rest of us shifters, for her skin is a golden shade of caramel. And she is also one not even from this planet! An alien, you say you are mated to an alien! I have seen her with my own eyes, she is nothing special. I think future alpha that you are making a terrible mistake here. My prince." She bowed, hoping and fluttering her lashes that he believed her poisonous, sneering words.

"I suppose you think you are? That doesn`t surprise me!" Clay said. "Well, I...."

"Come on Clay Star is right, and she would make a good match with you now Char, bless her loving, kind soul is on a different plain. A perfect match indeed." His mother argued.

She was supposed to be on his side Clay fumed.

"I would rather light my genitals on fire!" And he actually would.

"Clay..." His father warned him, as both Star and his mother gasped greatly offended by him. "But my petal, he is right. Not about the genital lighting though, Star isn`t that bad!" His dad chuckled and winked at him. "But about Hope. She is his fated mate darling...."

"So?"

"So! We are fated mates for goodness sake here petal, so you of all people should understand that they are souls destined ones and they belong together! Just only Imagine if I had been matched with another female instead of with you, even though we are fated mates, and then myself taken from you. You would have been outraged and so would I!"

His mother's eyes grew bright at that comment, and she growled possessively over her many years mate.

"Mine!" His mother's wolf hollered, trying to break through her control.

You didn't threaten to take an queens king, ever!

The beta`s daughter spoke.

"But this is different your majesty`s, me and Clay would go perfectly with each other. And I would make a good wife and mother to him and his son. And too our future children."

Clay growled at the disrespect to Hope. The thought of having children with Star made his skin crawl, even if he hadn`t found Hope it would have

He would protect her at all costs, and he didn't give a shit who knew it, he would shout it from the palace roof tops! He protected those that he cared about. Especially her.

His Hope. Just thinking of her made his heart leap.

"Mind your own Star, this had nothing to do with you." He warned in a husky voice his wolf trying to break the surface and release itself to them all. To dominate everyone that got in his and his mates path.

"And yes, he is right what exactly has this got to do with you Star?" The king said with a deep authoritative voice. "This is private royal business we are meant to be having, and as far as I am aware, you are not royalty or likely to ever be, given Clays wishes."

Star was not happy at that!

"I am sorry your highness. But was it not only a few months ago that beings from another planet took his highness, and some of the family far away to another planet entirely? And we have only just got them back here. And now his female, this Hope, who he claims is his mate is an alien too don't you forget it! How do we not know that she has cruel intentions in her heart, like that of the blue beings from Hazguard do. She could be in league with them!?

"You lie! She is nothing like those beasts!" Clay spat out angrily. Boy he was raging now. How could anyone be compared to those hideous things that crept out of the shadows from their cold ice planet. If he was king, then Stars head would have been lopped off and put on a stick for all those that imposed to see and fuck all the consequences!

Dark coarse fur started revealing itself on Clays toned thick, manly arms, and his eyes shone out bright in warning that he was more than a little pissed and his wolf was as well! Teeth became sharply chiselled fangs, and he snarled deeply at Star in warning, causing her to jump back from him in alarm.

His wolf started to emerge out of his dark handsome face causing his features to sharpen into something unique. He tried to stop it though with every ounce that he could muster, to reign his beast in for now, and remained there as a magnificent half beast and half man in warning to her. He wouldn`t let himself lose control over a lesser being then him!

He was going to be king; he controlled his wolf not the other way round!

But then fear enveloping him suddenly knocked him out of his enraged anger at the interfering female, Star. And it wasn't his own no, It was someone else`s fear that he felt in waves running through him!

"Some things wrong!" He snarled out. But what? What was wrong?

His wolf did as his master wanted and retreated back into his body where he belonged, and Clay moved. He ran like a shot, his huge, thick set muscly body running to Hope. He raced down the vastly shiny and decorated corridor leading to the main stairway, and he raced up what felt to him like a million stairs in the palace, they were never ending!

He didn't even have to know what room Hope was in, for although he know as he had told the assistant where to put her, he could smell her every increasing panicked scent, and her distress he would sense through his thick body, from miles upon miles away.

She screamed loudly, the sound could smash glass with the urgency of it.

He didn't bother knocking to enter her room, he wasn't that polite, no he wasn`t. He instead barged the door wide open with the power within his self, and nearly taking the poor wooden door off the hinges, with his strength.

Hope from behind the door somewhere gasped in her surprise at the sudden and fearful intrusion from him, added to her current distress.

"Hope, Hope what is wrong!" He bellowed loudly in a deep and scratchy voice, which was his caused by his wolf reaching the surface, at its mate's obvious distress. The wolf was more panicked as Hope did not have a wolf that his wolf could communicate with.

He stopped in front of her now. He paused at her in front of him and looked puzzled. He scratched his head confused for just a moment.

She was crying softly in front of the Large decorated mirror, on the far side of the room. He could see that oddly for some reason, where she had gotten them, he did not know, that she had a pair of sharp hair cutting scissors in one hand, and there was hair littering all over the floor in a fan, and she had taken her beads out of it, so it was set free onto her lean shoulders.

"Your hair Hope, what have you done to your hair? Why are you screaming my Hope, are you ok? I was worried!" He was confused, as the last time that they had spoken she had had jet black hair like his people did, and now instead it was a shade of golden brown, the colour of autumn leaves that shined in the sun, like that was beaming through the open window.

His people all had various shades of black hair to match their skin or grey hair sometimes, as they slowly became older and aged. They were quite an advanced species on their planet and had the means to dye hair if they so wished, but apart from youngsters using hair mascaras to brighten up a streak of two of their hair to be bold or to act different, no one really bothered with hair dye. The majority liked being who they were in their natural way.

They all embraced each other in their own uniqueness.

She glared at him, her tears drying now on her face now that her calmness was there to help her.

"I have done nothing to it Clay, why would I? It was black one minute, and now it is this golden-brown colour. I have not dyed it I promise, for I have only just arrived here, and it was not the suns doing, I am aware of that. I would not have come here if I would have known this planet was going to do things to me, that I didn't want. For why am I here anyway? When you will go ahead and find a new mate soon, and then I will be stuck watching my friend alone and unwanted from the sidelines..."

" But I.... "

"But you what? You asked me to come back with you for a while when the ship came to rescue you. And I agreed as I needed time away from home, to clear my head from what happened to Maya and I..." She wiped a lone tear from her face with her hand. Thinking of Maya`s death was so agonising still to her.

She continued on as he listened eagerly to her sinful voice. He could listen to her just talk for hours about anything and be enthralled, and they were both dominant people. Yes, he had to be as future alpha and king, but she was the only one who he would ever willingly want to submit to. Well except his parents of course, as he was not disrespectful. They had both brought him up from just a pup and were also who ruled the roost on this world.

And them alone.

Hope carried on confronting him in a harsh tone.

"And what was that zapping that went on between us earlier? You know what it was didn't you? But you wouldn't say. It was not the usual zapping that I can do with my palms in self-defence like my people can, but a sizzling zap when we both touched. Am I cursed somehow? Is what happened to my friend Maya, my fault? She asked in a whisper, her brown eyes glistening with her unshed tears.

"No." He said moodily. He growled at her in his anguish. How could he tell her the truth? Would she want him anyway?

He had to say something though, that was inevitable. "I am not ready to tell you, but I will in time. And no, it is nothing that you have done. Maya`s death was not your fault it was those ghastly aliens the Hazguard s. Listen my grandmother who is my father's mother, she has let's say certain magic in her like my sister has some of. She can sense things in people and will maybe be able to help us find out what has happened to your hair. And why it has changed. I promise you."

He leant over and ran his fingers through her now lightened brown hair. He wasn`t sure what had happened if he was honest to himself and her, but he liked her and what she looked like did not matter to him in the slightest. She could be balding, or have bright green hair, and he would still think that she was the prettiest girl out there in existence. Because beauty was only skin deep after all, and everyone was truly different to each other like they should be.

He supposed that there must be a reasonable explanation behind it all. He just hoped that nothing else changed for her. Not because he wouldn`t like it no, but as he didn't want to see his mate upset any more, and her black beaded hair, had meant something to her.

"Will she say why we spark when we touch?" She asked him hopefully, her face lighting up with hope.

He blushed feeling awkward, as he knew and didn't need his grandmother or anyone else to tell him the reason why.

"I am not sure she will, we will find out." He said to her now rather guiltily.

She knew with his whole-body language and change in stature that he was withholding information yet again from her, but she was not sure truthfully what or why he was.

She let out a small, exaggerated sigh and frowned, so that he would know that she was pissed off at him and his truth withholding ways.

He feeling bad, he did. He kissed her gently on the forehead in a sweet gesture, sending a spark zapping between them like a force as he pulled her to him in a sweet caress, and he hugged her oh so tightly to him, to him in both a possessive and caring manner.

His eyes crinkled in his happiness as at last he had found his love, and although they was not yet aware of it, but their hearts now beat the same tune as each other's did.

"Come." He took her hand firmly but gently with his own, and he led her out of the room, he led her through the palace, as she marvelled at all the wonders of the place and finally forgetting her freakishly changing by itself hair colour.

He said. "We will find my parents, and I will let them know all is well with you as I shot off from our meeting all of a sudden. And then I will give you a private tour of the town. Do you remember when you gave me a tour of yours? All the sights that we saw and trying to keep poor Ruddy from shining his yellow eyes brightly. You said stop that Ruddy every time his eyes changed until he started learning to keep them the same shade more when people where about! He laughed.

She also laughed out loud at the memory of it. When they had first met a few months ago though it seemed more, then he had stood there at her friends door which she had answered, looking for his beloved son. Stood there at the door waiting for an invite in, in no more than a loincloth that barely covered what it was supposed to cover!

She had been truly horrified at this fit, dark stranger at the door, but also rather impressed by him and curious about him and his strange but pleasing scent that wafted through the day air. He had smelt so good and still did to this day...

She had shown him, his sister Shelly and his son Ruddy around town. Gladly, whilst hoping that no one knew that the trio were all secretly wolf shifters from another planet. Though she supposed to him in his eyes, where she was from was not as exciting as this planet. She knew that he admired it and had tried with most of the people that he had met, for her sake.

As they walked on towards where he suspected that his parents were, then some workers stopped what they were doing as they saw them both approach. And they downed their tools as though on a break when they were just being nosy, they guessed.

A young lad maybe a blossoming teen, approached them carefully and whilst watching Clay cautiously. He bowed his head and lowered it is his submission, and fiddled his hands nervously in front of him, as if he was afraid of overstepping the mark to his prince.

And in front of what the workers guessed was the princes new female at that.

"Prince, our future Alpha. You are back home, and you are safe. I would just like to say that we are all so very happy for you. We are sorry to hear of Charmain, it was heard through the grapevines. We will honour her memory always future prince. But also, if you don't mind me saying, we are pleased as it looks like you have been blessed with a fated mate at long last! And welcome to you!"

The lad turned and beamed at Hope with a warm welcome. Clay growled lightly in warning at another male nearing his mate. For she was his!

The shifters she had seen so far seemed to be all good, hard-working people.

"Thank you." She said politely to the lad who smiled enthusiastically at her. But at his words, inside her heart dropped. A fated mate what did he mean by that? Clay didn't have a fated mate, did he? And it wasn't her or he would have told her...

"Thank you Dub. I don't suppose you know where the king and queen are?" Clay said to the lad nodding his head. He looked at Hope and knew that what Dub had said was making her feel uneasy.

"In the royal gardens sire." Dub backed away.

"Thank you."

"You are most welcome sire." And with that the workers looked at Dub like he was either brave or stupid for his outspokenness, and they all carried on back with what they were doing. The two mates, carried on walking.

"Hope I" ... But he was interrupted suddenly by the sounds of what she assumed was a wolf or more howling, and then an extremely loud roaring sound then a loud bang as though a shot gun had gone off.

Some armed warrior guards ran past them, on the way to the royal gardens too. Some in their normal form, and a few were in wolf form. All shades of black, grey or brown fur and some a mixture. Each wolf seemed to Hope as unique as the people all were.

"What`s going on?" She asked him concerned by the ruckus outside.

He hurried her along with a gentle nudge, and then stopped suddenly, his feet firmly to the ground as a large no humongous form caused a shadow in the sky above, and a loud roaring sound emitted from whatever it was.

Clay stopped with her, as not wanting to lead her into danger, even though he knew outside is where he should be with the people who needed him, he couldn't lead his mate into charters unknown.

He tried to reassure Hope, who he thought would be quivering in fear by the roaring above, but who actually looked like if she could grab a sword and fight as well! "It will be ok Hope. It sounds like a dragon has got loose from the mountains don't you worry!"

"A dragon?" She had never heard of a dragon. It sounded loud and scary, but she as ever her usual self was curious more than scared.

"Yes. A dragon. They are enormous creatures, and they fly wild here, but they normally keep their-selves to the hills, and they are not allowed in this housed area in the city. They are ok with our normal form it does not bother them, but they do not like us at all in wolf form, and they normally keep away from this built-up area. They prefer the silence from out there and not here. They also breath fire as well." She gasped at that. Wow!

"How do they know not to; do you tell them? Can they talk? And fire, wow! Sounds dangerous." She was desperate to see one for herself, with her own eyes.

"No, no don't be silly of course they can't talk!" He laughed at the thought of a talking dragon in their city. His female cracked him up, with her ways and words sometimes!

"And yes, they can be dangerous, if they drift towards the habited parts of the city. They as I said, like the mountains and volcano's. Higher up places, and these areas here are too low, and populated for their usual liking.

She observed the handsome male beside her. The wolf man.

"Well, you have talking wolves here, aren't there? so why not dragons that speak to you? Come on, we should go help, Clay. You cannot always protect me from danger. We need to see what is going on, and you are the prince so by rights you should be out there in the thick of it and helping."

"I fear that you are right my Hope." He smiled warmly as he knew that she was.

She took his hand urgently again, ignoring the light sparking between them and they continued towards the outside, and also the roaring.

As they reached the gardens finally, the noise from outside became over whelming. Hope put her hands over her ears, and she could see in front of them what obviously used to be beautiful gardens for the royals to walk in, and to relax on lazy evenings and orchards full of various strange to her fruits, was now a charred mess from the dragon flying angrily above them, in a great whirlwind of rage. It was red and beautiful with thick scales all over, and it had a mad look in its huge round staring eyes, like it was gone in the head.

Wolves shifted back to their person form as it seemed to antagonise the dragon further like Clay had said, when they were in their animal form. Fire flew out of its mouth at an alarming rate, and smoke blew out of its noise while it breathed in and out, with a loud and unpleasant snorting sound.

"Wow." Hope said looking at the stunning red creature before them both amazed and in awe of it.

"Beautiful, but deadly. Like someone else that I know well." Clay said. He turned to a warrior guard near him, who was frantically trying to put a large and increasing fire out frightfully too near to the palace, and others ran out with various hoses and large buckets. Clay truthfully was not sure what to do in this situation, as in his three decades or so on this planet, then the dragons had kept to their selves, and they so kept to theirs.

The species respected each other's areas.

"Rogues!" He muttered out loud, for what else could have driven the large spectacular beasts out of the comfort of their home in the mountains, and driven them close to his people, where they so usually always had avoided? But then could even rogues, or those with knowledge drive the beasts from their nests, and from their precious treasures?

"Let's help." Hope said, and they walked over to where his parents were frantically sending out orders to all their people. His mother shrieked as they approached for them to stay well back, and his father pulled his mate behind him so that he could shield his precious queen, as the fiery beast looked right at them all in the eye with its large ones, and it landed swiftly in the queens most prized flowerbed. Knocking all her hard worked precious flower's over!

"Stay back please, I beg of you!" Clay whispered in Hopes small, curved ear. Not that she ever listened to him, for she was a fine but strong and independent woman who listened to no one. Except herself of course.

They were all obviously worried about the carnage that the dragon had brought to the palace with its fiery body, but none could have foretold what it did so next.

For the red like blood dragon, eyed Hope like she was a prize to it, and approached her gently and curiously with its snout blowing out thin steam. Clay still stood in its way much to its rage, but it tried barging with all its huge might past him to get to her. Clay had to bring his wolf to the front to keep power and strength running through his veins, to let the power surge as much as he could without transforming, as he didn't want to rile the beast.

This creature before him would not beat him and he hope that it knew that.

Only one creature would ever get him on his hands and knees, and she was standing right next to him.

He would not let the beast have his one, he would slit its giant pulsing throat and mount its large head onto the castle walls in a warning to others not to cross him, before he would ever let her be injured or taken away from him while he was still breathing the planets air!

"No!" Clay screamed at the dragon again in warning, and he tried and pushed it with all his strength. It snarled at him snapping its huge teeth which were like spikes with the size of them all. He couldn't even shift into his wolf where most his strength lay in his impressive wolf form, as it would make the dragon even more wound up by it! His best guard threw him a large, curved sword, and he held it menacingly at the beasts face, his eyes glowing yellow in his built-up anger at it.

At the danger to his princess.

But it surprised them all and stopped where it had landed in its path on the now damaged flower bed, and It looked at Hope, with a strange calm expression lit across its normally fierce face. And it lowered its head to her as though it was submitting to her and let out a loud purr like noise! Like she was familiar to it!

"What is happening here Clay?" Hope whispered behind his thick back, as she could not see much with the large, dark, excruciating handsome man protecting her, like he was a knight in shining armour.

"I do not know, if I am honest here." He drawled to her.

The dragon at last managed to nudge Clay out of the way much to his horror, and it seemed for reasons unknown to anyone to be adamant that it wanted to get to Hope!

She looked at the stunning beast before them with great puzzlement, lit over her golden skinned face.

"It's ok Clay. Let me." She said.

She tried to get round him to get to the beast that was enthralled by her like she was its own hoard of gold, but Clay ignored her, and he was trying his hardest not to shift right there! She was his! His mate! He would tear the dragon limb from limb with his sword and then with his claws if it so much as burnt even a small piece of her caramel skin.

She moved round him, and reached out a hand shakily, and touched the fine now settled dragon on the head gently, whilst also carefully observing its body language for any signs that it was going to breath out fire again. And in her direction at that! But it didn't thankfully to her relief. She didn't wanna be toasted all the way through, like a big fat marshmallow on a stick!

It seemed to enjoy her stroking it softly with her smooth hands, and it eyed her non-stop and then it made one last purr and backed off, and it lifted its huge self-up, and then flew back to the mountains where it came from, as though it was never even there, and they had all dreamed it in their sleep!

The fire that had been raging through the vast gardens that had been getting out of control, and the burnt-out orchards was now out, and the guards and people that had come to help all stopped and gawped openly at Hope.

His parents followed behind the crowd. Gawping at her rudely as well like she had too heads. She felt uncomfortable at all the peoples gazes upon her, like she had done something wrong when she had touched the beasts lethal but cute snout with a gentle tender hand.

"This has never happened before." The queen said abruptly in her disbelief and shaking her strong head side to side.

The king nodded his agreement and shrugged carelessly.

He let his dominating wife do most of the talking as per usual unless, it was expected of him. It was their way and it worked well for them. Clay had always found it weird his mother being more in control then his father. That was until he met Hope that is.

"What had never happened?" Hope asked from the side-lines meekly. "Clay, did you see the beast? It was amazing wasn't it! You are so lucky, to have such a creature such as that one on your planet!" She squealed happily, and excited at her first seeing a magnificent dragon.

Touching the large vicious to start with beast had been frankly terrifying for her of course it had, she felt like the beast would be friendly, she could see it in its beautiful eyes. But she didn't know for sure.

But anyway, it had also been simply amazing!

She wondered when and if the creature would be back to the city for a visit. They could name it! Or did it already have one? It couldn't speak so no one would ever know it...

Clay explained.

"The dragon. No one has ever petted a dragon before to my knowledge. Except you." Clay said awkwardly, feeling stunned at what he and the others around him, had just witnessed on that day with his mate.

It had unsettled him. His mate was already an out-worlder, wolf less, he didn't want anyone thinking she was any more different to them.

For the dragons if disturbed did sometimes fly around the city yes, and a few on very rare occasions had caused mayhem before when disturbed in their nests but they kept away from the people in the main city, and the people kept away from them. The creatures got riled by their wolf form, so they knew to avoid shifting near one for fear of an outraged attack.

"What do you mean never?" She said and waited for an answer. Did he mean what she thought he meant?

He looked at her, his yellow eyes twinkling and growled lightly.

"I mean, it has never happened here at the palace, never Hope."

She understood him now. She was stunned into silence.

"Something is amiss." His mother faced Clay and frowning. She looked at Hope and said, "Your hair. Wasn't it black before? But how?"

"We don't know why." Hope said quietly.

She thought coming with Clay to his home planet would be an adventure, and it had been that all right after only a day of being there, but it also seemed full of drama too. And she didn't like drama much.

A gorgeous warrior female came out and stood near the front, and she looked at Hope in blatant disgust. It was written all over her face. She openly sneered at her like she was disgusting.

"Yes, can I help you?" Hope asked the woman curiously and acting not intimidated by the strange female, who obviously had issue with her. She wasn't scared of whoever she was, who seemed to think for some reason that she was the queen bee.

The female went to speak back to Hope, but Clay cut her off sternly and sharply.

"Not now, Star."

"But she..."

"I said, not now Star." He said slowly for enthusiast. His beast was slowly getting fed up with the betas daughter meddling in his affairs, and her meddling was annoying him as well!

She lowered her head to him. "Yes, future Alpha." She wasn't pleased it was evident, by her shocked mannerisms.

Clay spoke to his parents.

"Alpha, Luna. We are going to travel to see Grandmother. I have a few questions for her. That I think only she can answer for us."

"Answers to what?"

"Mother, father. I think that Hope is the golden one from the prophecy. The one to bring us all together. "

Everyone stopped what they were doing, everyone stopped talking amongst themselves and looked astonished, and gasped loudly muttering to themselves, and they all stopped and looked at Hope, and turned her neck and she looked at him.

What was a golden one? And why was everyone staring at her like she had stood in shit?

She looked down now and her skin glowed a shade of gold, and then disappeared back to normal.

What the!

CHAPTER THREE

After getting roped into pack duties like he had never even been away from there in the first place, Clay went off and tried to find Hope, excitement in his heart and nerves deep in his soul. She had gone back to her room back in the palace where they were currently staying for some time, she said she wanted time to think stuff over, and to process certain things.

He hadn`t wanted to let her go off by herself to ponder with her ever winding thoughts alone, but she had insisted to her prince that she needed space, and some alone time after the tiring journey. And anyway, his parents had asked him to come along with them to sort some important things out that needed doing.

He had sighed, things were back to normal already!

He had responsibility more than she could ever know though.

He thought that on the look on Hopes face that she also found his mother rather overbearing, which if Clay was being brutally honest, she kinda was so!

Apparently according to what his parents had relayed, a few rogues had been sighted on the outskirts of their great magnificent city, and that to them could mean that trouble was on the horizon. He wondered what they wanted this time from them and prayed and hoped that they didn't eventually learn of Hope`s arrival to their planet, and that nobody found out who she was to him.

As it could put her in grave danger.

And if they done anything untoward to her, then he would have to then go onto destroy them. For she was now his to protect, and his alone. For she was his destiny.

The outcasts normally stayed hidden away in the shadows on the outskirts of the city or into the next towns. That was because, well it was their fault anyway that they had been banned from the city, as they had refused to join any pack that was offered to them, so if they lost out on the luxury's that his people were all afforded, then it was their own fault really.

And he wouldn`t let himself feel sorry for any of them.

Nope. In his eyes, they all deserved everything that went their way.

He had struggled to be able to concentrate at the meeting that the royals had earlier, he would shamefully have to admit. He had never broken his concentration like that at an important meeting before, but then he had other pressing things on his mind. Like a tall, lean, alluring other world female.

But he didn't curse inside, and he knew that he needed to do his job properly for the benefit of the main pack. And all the others that were out there too! He couldn't let himself get distracted by romance, when they all relied on him for authority alongside his parents side.

He would need to gradually learn in time, to be able to juggle all of his multiple essential responsibilities, and also Hope. And to prove to them all that he would be the king that they all needed him to be. And the one they deserved, unlike now.

And to do them all so very proud.

He approached her tastefully decorated room that he had picked himself for her as it was near him, and to her taste, and he knocked gently on the door to her room with a fist. He ignored his wolf whining from inside his soul to be let out and to be free with the world, and who also gravely more than anything wanted him to throw open the door to her room, and to rip it off its hinges, to get to the woman he loved as quickly as possible. To mate her, to claim her at last in the only way possible. Through rutting.

Loved. Wow did he truly love her?

But of course, he did. Beyond anything, and anyone in the world. Excluding Ruddy.

From the moment that he had thankfully managed to escape from his alien forced stinky ass prison and had gone with his big sister to search for his lost son, and found her keeping careful watch of his boy, then he had been infatuated by her and her entire being.

He had wanted her for his own. And he still did.

His sons first shift into his wolf had back then gone horribly wrong, and he had horrifyingly become stuck as half beast and half in his normal form. Which had never happened to a wolf shifter before, ever... And he hoped that his son had managed to fix what had needed fixing and was safe and well when he had escaped and had found some good people to aid him.

And to protect him back then, when he so couldn`t.

His son had been too inexperienced unlike him and his sibling to manage to be able to hide his personal scent as he roamed the planet where they were held in the search of freedom, so they had with no trouble following his young trail for a few mile or so first in their wolf form, then finally in their normal form, when they too had eventually gotten away from the blue beasts.

They had lost their prisoner clothes along the way with a startling rip when they had transformed into their inner animals and had only managed to salvage their underwear from it. They were out of practise!

So, he had bravely knocked on Hope`s door after following Ruddy`s scent there, and both most definitely impressed her, and also no doubt probably traumatised her when she opened the door to a big, black, thick and tall, delicious male like nobody she had seen before, or would likely ever see again standing there in just what resembled a loin cloth.

A small one at that. The loin cloth not what lay in it.

She had made him laugh at first meeting each other, as one of her first words to him had been -

"Um. I`m not sure how to ask, but why are you wearing just little pants? Not that it's not nice to look at! I mean you got the goods for it just wondering..." Hope had stuttered and stammered back then on sight blatantly embarrassed by his near and obvious nudity. She had tried at the time to stop looking at his manly body that interested her so very much, but he was eager for her to continue to look at him, to admire him. And she had done so.

If he had not been there at her door after news of his son, then he would of maybe have taken her for his mate then and there, as she had riled him up so! But that was then, and this is now.

Hope groaned loudly from behind the door at his urgent knocking and opened it in a hurry whilst muttering under her breath about ever, impatient males.

She peered her head round the door like the first time that they had met, eyeing him with simply confusion on her stunning golden skinned face at seeing him standing there, when she had told him otherwise.

"Clay, I thought that we both agreed that you would give me some time and space, now that we were here. To try to work out what the heck is going on with me right now! I feel like a freak!" She let out a hiss on speaking the words.

"Never!" He growled his fangs trying to push through his gums. "Don't say those words ever, my one." His eyes flashed bright in his warning, teetering at the edge of unexplained madness by his mates distress.

Wolf shifters especially the males were protective over their mates fated or arranged mates.

She sighed then shrugged her slim shoulders in defeat.

"Well come in, I have made some fresh juice from that little cold cupboard that you have over there."

"It is what is known as a fridge." He replied simply.

"Where I am from, we didn't have these fridges, or even this so called electric that you have here. Where I am from, they have barely anything."

She continued on explaining, but he was aware from his time there.

"We didn't have any of this like you do." She said waving her hand out in enthuses at all the magnificent things that the room held.

The difference in planet`s was plain to see.

It was all so very confusing to her. She was like a mere peasant compared to the vast obvious wealth of the prince shifter sat beside her, and the vast palace that they were staying in for the time being. It was magnificent.

He shrugged not caring for her life of poorness no longer, as he would now always only look after her and her needs now and forever, as long as she breathed the planets air. It didn't mean nothing to him anymore.

"You do now. You can have whatever you want from here. Whenever you want. I would give you the world"

She blushed. "So how exactly are we getting to your grandmothers location? Are we walking. or using a transport cart?" She gently pondered.

"Well, we have jet gliders here as you saw when we walked here to the palace, but we prefer to walk most places or run as our wolves. I myself, don't like jet gliders personally."

He shuddered not liking the blasted things at all, whilst pacing the room and thinking over things at the same time.

"Why don't you like them, if they get you where you need to be? It would save getting tired feet!" She wondered by his noticeable wincing if the fierce and noble shifter, was actually scared of something? No, no way!

He tried to explain carefully to her whilst also trying to keep his dignity intact.

"I fell off one as a child when I was joyriding on one, and I fell off and crashed into something hard. I nearly broke my neck in the great fall from the sky, I had been at great height when I crashed. I managed to heal quickly thank goodness with my wolf healing, and then some potion created by the fairies."

"Oh my. I am just glad to hear that you were ok in the end!" She exclaimed. "But what are Fairies?" She asked him.

"Fairies are little flying magical creatures. Their dust and also their corpses, give off various and different magical abilities, but you are strictly prohibited to ever harm one when they are alive, as like the dragons they are a protected species. And their dust you must find for yourself or be given to by one. Plus, if you harm one even just accidentally then you don't want to see the fairies wrath, for when they eventually come for you with their family following not far behind them. They can be extremely evil little things, and they also have really sharp teeth, and a firm grip when they clamp down with them. My dad had to bargain with one for the dust, an expensive price to save his son. Like any parent would try and do."

"Oohh sounds like it was a nasty business. At least you got given some of the dust to help you in the end though Clay. That I am forever thank full of." She beamed at him. "Shall we walk to your grandmothers then, if you have some fears from the jets? I don't mind whatever we do, if it suits you, Clay."

She shrugged smiling warmly at him, which surprisingly giving him unexpected butterflies in his six packed stomach. A wolf prince with butterflies from a woman, who would have thought of it!

She commanded him. "Anyway. Now sit-down Clay because I want you to tell me exactly what a golden one is, and we aren`t leaving for your grandmothers until you have done so."

CHAPTER FOUR

"No."

"No?"

"No."

"What do you mean no, Clay!"

"I meant exactly what I said."

"But why?"

"Just not here, my Hopey. Not right now. This isn`t the right place, for what needs to be said. And anyway, we need way more privacy than we are ever going to get here for what we have to do. I really want to show you something. Something that is special to me, and for me alone. It is an exquisite room down the other end of the palace. It`s magnificent, you will have to see for yourself. Come with me, Hopey."

She eyed him warily like he was plotting to do a murder or something, as he was acting extremely suspicious right then and he was being cryptic with his words again...

She sighed. Why couldn't he just spit it out what he meant! What blardy room!

He secretly admired and loved that she could give as good as she got with him, and that she did not simply roll over and take whatever he so commanded, and just to take it! When they had first met on her world, he had thought for a fleeting but only fleeting moment, that she might have been too dominant for someone such as him, who was an alpha heir by his blood, and who was soon in the not-too-distant future to be in charge of things.

The ruler of them all....

But actually, he had found out to his pleasure from watching all her unique mannerisms and ways and from spending quality time just with her, that he was enjoying the challenge of her dominant nature, and her strong-willed manners.

She had power of her own. To him. He would actually go as far as to obey her every command to keep her staying happy, and to keep her there on his planet, and there by his side. For always.

And besides, he wouldn`t ever want to dampen her feisty spirit and weaken her, by making her into something that she was not. She was who she was, and he was who he was.

Different, but meant to be.

And the moon goddess was never wrong with her choices, was she? But then he had noted to himself that even the rogues had fated mates, except for they were normally as deranged as their mate so was so that didn't mean much! The moon goddess normally picked her matches well and made them a good fit to each other's very existences. But he was to his knowledge and his parents, the first Triumph shifter to be mated to an off worlder that he knew of or had ever heard of in their lifetime.

That could mean some shifters had mates that weren't even of his world! The discovery of Hope being his mate could lead to problems like others wanting to go off world in search for them! It was too dangerous after they had learnt of the evil, barbaric Hazguard`s existence. Beings who wanted to take over all...

She put her hands onto her lean but oh so curved hips and glowered at him in her teasing warning. She wasn't letting him take her whatever the heck he wanted without a say in it!

"It had better not be your bedroom that you are showing me to buddy, or else I`m staying here, thank you very much!" A smile threatened to break free from her face.

He laughed at that remark, at his mate with her one-track filthy dirty mind! His eyes twinkled happily, and he grinned broadly at her his smile beaming out. The little she-devil. She kept him on his toes, and oh how he liked it! He wished to the gods that he was right that moment showing her his bedroom, but if he did then she wouldn`t want to leave there any time once he had had his way with her!

She would be begging to stay.

For he would when the time was right, take her to great heights so that she soared high into orgasm heaven, and then back down again with an enjoyable crash. And repeat.

His eyes twinkled mischievously at that.

"Well, my Hope, my bedroom is I have to admit rather magnificent for you to see. Especially the very large, new four-poster bed that is currently in there on my orders, and waiting for my new mate to lay down on it, naked, legs spread..." He winked looking at her like he was the hungry, drooling wolf and that she was the three little piggies-he was wide-eyed with his hunger, and ever need for her, and for her existence alone.

He reached over and took her twitching smaller than his hand gently with his large one, entwining their fingers together, and he loved now how they tingled in tune whereas before it had frightened him with the passing shocks that he received every time they had brushed skin with each other. He hadn`t been ready for what was to come then, no, but he was heading for it now quicker than he had thought he would be!

For he was by nature an impatient male.

She looked at him her eyes low, with a slight pinkish glowing blush appearing on her golden brown soft like caramel skin. And he simply loved the fact of how close they were now, and the way that they both brought peace and joy to each others lives. He shivered in anticipation. He would fuck her so gently when she was his beloved queen he so would, but he also would fuck her so hard that she would not be able to walk straight after, to take her like the wolf that he was when she was his Luna.

He sniffed smelling something tantalising reaching his senses. It smelt good whatever it was inhaling. What was that? Oh. Oh, It was that he could smell her arousal again, it must be that! Wow, she smelt fine, he thought cheekily to himself enjoying her fine scent wafting through his nose and committing it to his memory bank. knowing that the secret that she did not know he had such sharp a sense of smell even in person form, or that he could scent personal things like that.

If she did ever know then he could guarantee that she would surely be embarrassed right, then at what he was currently drooling at! He could eat her lovely cunt alive and go back to it every day for another taste.

She looked at him and frowned at his increasingly suspicious look and wondering why he was looking at her like that and why she imagined that he had a naughty glint lingering there in his pale-yellow eyes. And she tilted her head to the side, whilst fiddling with her new hairstyle nervously. And she wondered again for the billionth time, what the devilishly delicious male in front of her, was thinking or scheming about. With the bold smirk appearing on his face and licking his thick dark lips with a large rough tongue, and the lust starting to cloud over his eyes then it was something surely no good that he was contemplating!

Typical males and their one-track minds she thought! She would love to be able to read his mind. Would he be thinking of her? She doubted it. His mate was out there for him somewhere.... Sigh. She tried to ignore her lingering jealousy. From what she had been told by Clay was the moon goddess

She bet though her mind wondering into the unknown, that he was amazing in bed though with his thick luscious curious fingers, and his large delicious thick tongue that he licked his lips within a naughty but innocent manner, whilst raising a lone brow at her teasingly. She wondered if would everything else on his body be so large? Of course, it would. For everything else about him was really rather large, and she had had a sneak peek through the tiny loin cloth that he had worn at their first meeting.

And she believed he was packing it down there!

Not now Hope! Not now! She thought scolding herself, feeling incredibly angry with herself, at her mind drifting to dirty thoughts when they simply needed some answers to her current predicament. Like her golden hair and the tingles on touching each other. But she did have a strange unwanted feeling in her soul, that he did In fact know the reason for all the shocks on them touching, and so did his parents she guessed, but he for some reason was keeping his cards hidden from her....

She looked him up and down, taking his whole sense in. For he was bloody simply put-gorgeous!

For yes, he might be a dark and dashing wolf shifter prince, and also soon to be king of them all until he met his death, but she knew that she for some unknown reason that she was the one who was in control here she reckoned so, and he had better darn well know it and abide by it!

She finally spoke and shook herself out of her awkward silence.

She waggled a finger at him.

"If it's your nether regions and bedroom you are taking me to see my great and respectable wolf princee, then much as I`m sure they are both rather nice for one to look at and to enjoy then for many hours, then it's a bit inappropriate of you to mention to me, prince Clay." She bowed her head mockingly, knowing she could get away with it with it being just the two of them! No sire, or prince! But equals.

He chuckled at the image of it. She cracked him up she truly did!

"No, unfortunately it is not." He drawled in that alluring voice of his. "And if it was then you wouldn`t want anything else on the whole and entire planet! Come now. This way." He gestured to the door.

He reached over her curvy figure, and he naughtily stole a bottle of water out of the chilled under counter fridge that was meant for Hope and Hope alone, and sneakily took a big thirsty gulp then a large guzzling swig, so some ran down his thick lips. He licked them clean. He threw the rest over his face to cool himself down from the heat.

Then he led her gracefully out of the room, and through the long palace corridors.

She had never in her twenty-six years had the pleasure of being in, or even seeing such a beautiful and large building with her very own eyes. It was a stunning place, it really was. A great deal of love and care had been put into its creation from what she could see. Where she lived back on her planet, then it was mainly small one or two-person cottages, or for larger needing households -family homes, but here the places had been made with complete and utter love and care, and she could tell the packs were well cared for by the royals, as even all the normal mere folk, had nice places to call their home.

Her town could learn a thing or two from the shifter people!

"We might as well have a brief tour while we are here Hope. We as you know lived here before the alien incident, but I was at the time in the middle of building me and Ruddy and Char our own house near the palace, for some privacy finally. When we, you know got taken that put wind to it..."

He scowled and growled angrily a bit too loudly, making Hope flinch at the fierce sounding noise from his thick lips, and jump back on edge at his behavior. She would never get used to his wolf losing control sometimes when it couldn't help it like that, and it trying to break free in its built-up anger, but she didn't think that Clay would ever hurt her intentionally.

It was scary sometimes when that happened, but she supposed that it was just who he was. For he was half wolf, and half man. Two souls in one body. It must be weird she thought to have a beast inside trying to take over at times.

Clay was understandably jarred off at himself at what happened back then with the alien abduction, even though it blatantly wasn't his fault that the aliens had taken them away before. And Hope had told him time and time again, in her gentle, loving reassurance that only the blue beasts were to blame. But it seemed to be to her annoyance to be rather slow to sink into his thick skin, that he wasn't at any fault. No one could have got away from them.

He had in Hopes opinion done all he could, for when the brutal aliens wanted something then they got what they wanted... Hope was all too aware of it, she had seen at first hand.

He had heard Ruddy screaming back then on that awful fearful day, that day which forever had caused a shiver going through his whole and entire soul, which would never leave him while he breathed Triumphs own air.

His young beloved son had only been out doing the usual things those young boys did on any planet- playing with their favorite toys and getting up to mischief behind their parent's unknowing backs.

Ruddy wasn't any different!

He, his sister and guards rushed over to where the fearful shrieks came from, and to their complete and utter disgust, out there in the open was a disgustingly tall, stinky, blue and brutal being that had their gorgeous, innocent, sweet son in its gross grasp, and it was spouting nonsense out of its thin blue lips, in a language that they did not know or understand.

They couldn't reason with the brute though they tried so they did, as they couldn't understand each others' languages and words in order to properly communicate with one another, and the alien had the upper hand, as unfortunately they could hypnotize their unsuspecting prey with their black, beady eyes. Plus, they also had magnificent made but scary looking stun guns, and numerous different fierce and depraved outer-world weapons that they liked smacking people with!

His heart had nearly stopped in his thick chest with his anguish, at what the alien could do to his precious boy when he had seen his son clutched in its freakish clawed hands, with a firm and clawed grip round his beloved boy. And to their detriment, not able to escape from it. Thankfully though they were all back now, so they would hopefully put that all past them and move forward, and now things had been set up by security and his parents to prevent an attack from the skies from ever happening again.

So now the aliens would remain just in his memory and keep away from the now.

His dad had told him at the meeting that a few months ago, yet another spaceship had turned up on the planet Triumph! Clay couldn't believe what he was hearing from him! But how? Another one, surely not! It this time though had crash landed hard onto their world and luckily for them it had contained only an earthling captain and his faithful crew.

It had been thanks to the earthling captain lord Raymond, who had told his parents where he guessed the aliens had gone to as they hadn`t been sure, that Clay himself had been rescued! For that one day he might be able to thank him in person for.

This Raymond had apparently helped his dad sort their best ship out for lift off, and he had helped him and his faithful crew to fix theirs, and then sent them on their merry way! As friends no, his father wouldn`t go as far as to say that. But as trusted associates- yes, definitely. After the Hazguard`s attack, it would take them a while to learn to like non shifter people, which is where Clay knew that Hope had a long road ahead of her. But he would be there by her side every step of the way! Because that`s what mates did do, wasn't it?

It had been unexpected, but they should have been prepared for it.

She praised him for she was proud of him. "You are so clever Clay, wow building a house all on your own, I could never do such a thing!" She was right she couldn't, with her small dainty hands. She thought that he must be an expert with his large hands, to build his own house all by himself...

"Yes, now me and my mate will live there with Ruddy." he said to her. "It is nearly time for it that I am now certain." He said also proud of what he had achieved. For why he would get others to build a home, when he could do it himself!

"Is that warrior from before, your mate? She seemed extremely posed and beautiful and also a warrior too! But a tad frighteningly jealous of you and other females, if I am not overstepping here now Clay."

He spat out. "Pah she so wishes!"

Hope felt relief at that answer. For the woman looking at her previously while nasty looking in soul was simply beautiful, a masterpiece. And also, a warrior and she had a wolf unlike her. She let herself think about something that she had never thought about before. Was she, his mate? She felt like she was at times and all the signs lately had been pointing to it, and she felt such a weird and powerful connection with him she truly did. But she couldn't be, could she? No, she could not let herself

He showed her where he was staying which he was right he did have a huge bed; she saw eyeing it nervously. He quickly showed her where Ruddy was staying also when there, his parent's quarters, kitchens, dining rooms, meeting rooms and the wolf and Triumph training rooms. And Ruddy`s study room.

Finally at long last as her head was spinning, he took a curved old key out and unlocked a large carved door with it.

"This is our private library." He gestured to the book lined room.

Wow. She gasped completely surprised, as he dragged her through the large inviting door, and into the large room crammed with all sorts of various books and locked the door behind them, whilst tilting his head and making sure no one was following them or seeing them go in.

People on Triumph were like any planet. They had their fair share of gossips.

She noticed the way that each room they saw were designed so she guessed in case they turned into their wolf whilst in it. Set up with plenty of room to shift into their beast in comfort and move around. Her room was smaller she felt uneasy at the fact she did not have a wolf.

She wondered what it would be like to have one. Probably weird if not used to it and would take some getting used to!

He noticed her sudden unease on entering the stunning book layered library, and so took her over to a large bookcase with a large welcoming sofa surrounding it, and beside it an amazing book nook, to hide out in. And he went over and picked up a large dusty, seen better days old book. He carefully handed it to her after wiping the dust off it gently with one hand, as it was so old and obviously remained untouched in a long while.

"This is the one here, Hopey. Look at this." He pointed.

She fidgeted on the spot. Would he still like her if he knew how dumb she was? Maybe? She ummed and arhed but then decided to tell him, as he would find out anyway soon enough!

She spoke not meeting his gaze.

"Clay, I.... I cannot read. We did not have these types of books where I am from. They are splendour itself." Which they were. She fingered through the old book, feeling the pages flicked between her fingers. It felt like home here in this library, comfortable and reliable. She could spend hours in a place like this, savouring the peace and quiet of the room.

He shrugged by her comment, not at all even bothered in the slightest by her statement. "We are both from different up bringing`s and from different worlds, and galaxies, Hope. I was aware of that before now. It does not matter to me that you cannot read these books, for I do not care at all, and it should not matter to you. And besides this book here has beautiful pictures that outline the stories that lay inside, so it does not need to be even read with words."

"Thank you." She loved his supportive nature; he was just a dream!

"I will read what you cannot my other one." He began to read the book to her.

"The golden one is prophesied to bring the wolves all together, and to bring their enemies the rogues, and the flying dragons back to the fold. The golden one will have a beautiful shade of golden-brown hair, and she will possess golden skin as you can see in this image." He pointed at the picture, beside the writing. He continued.

"With a golden magical eerie glow to her golden skin. When they arrive, they are supposed to unlock the ability for all to find their fated mate for themselves, and not just a few of the lucky ones. Oh no. But them all..."

"In a few circumstances, it had caused tragedy when a wolf had found a picked mate, and then later down the line their fated mate had turned up out of the blue. In one couple, one person rejected their picked mate, and another rejected their fated one which is just crazy." He sighed at the absurdly notion of it all!

She didn't know. "I do not understand this mate thing Clay. And I will never need one, which is a dear shame, but as you say a mate is surely for life, and not to be rejected like that. Like they are nothing..."

He nodded his head in agreement as she in his opinion was right and blushed at his secret that she did in fact have a fated mate, and now she forever always would. Him. His wolf hummed happily but silently from the inside at that feeling.

Now, he had met his one and only, he wondered how could anyone reject their own mate like that, when they were supposed to be fated to be? And to go ahead and defy the moon goddess in that way, it was simply an absurd notion that he would never understand!

As the moon started to glow high in the sky, and to be visible through the large, decorated library windows, she looked at him and his black skinned sexy perfection that she would never get tired of looking at, and then back at the large, old, dusty book, laying spayed out on the table. And she to her horror, lightly growled. She gasped in the shock and horror of it. What a weird sound!

His eyes widened on hearing her growl trickle through the spacious room, but he said nothing though and kept his face blank of any emotion. She just shook her head puzzled and thought that maybe as she was hanging around with wolves so much, that she was starting to act like one on being there with them all!

"Oops." She giggled in a non-lady like manner and put she her hand to her mouth whilst he then smirked at her embarrassment.

"Can I take this book to my room?" She asked.

She really wanted to know more about the legend, and it was getting to be late. She could maybe flick through the pictures in bed before she passed out for the night.

He placed a hand on hers and eyed her carefully. His heart thudding. His skin buzzing.

"Hope. You can do whatever you want whilst you are here, and I hope that you make this place your home, and that you decide to eventually stay here with us, as one of us. You know that is what I want, and what young Ruddy wants. But the choice must be yours, and yours alone."

She shrugged.

"I think I will need more time to figure stuff out like that. But I like what I see so far here, plus the view here in this beautiful room isn`t so bad." She lightly flirted with the shifter prince before her, whilst not knowing whether it was a clever idea to even go there.

He looked from his secret princess to round at the room that had captivated him from since when he was a small child. He had spent much time here studying and reading when he should have been out in the world playing like a normal child and doing normal things like the boy he had been. His mother had come into the library many times to scold him, and he learnt to hide from her much to her displeasure!

Like a mother and son game of hide and seek, but where the mother was getting slowly and slowly, more annoyed by her hiding all over the place wolf shifter son!

He spoke from the heart.

"Yes, the library is most impressive. I come here all the time when I need some time out from the cities people, plus I do read the odd book, bet you didn't know that! I came here a lot as a boy probably too much, learning about our heritage."

She teased him.

"I was not on about the library view. But that sounds amazing to have your own hidey-hole away from the others."

He openly blushed at her what he presumed was flirtatious comment, and his wolf felt content on realizing she had been teasing and flirting with him. That was a good sign! His heart fluttered happily. His cock swelled in his pants. He would have to fist it later when alone, to get rid of all the frustration that this female here left in his nether regions!

He tried to act cool.

"Yes, yes, it is. You can do whatever with the book, but it has other legends in there, and it needs to be either locked in here safely or be locked in your room. I do trust most of the people here but not enough to leave something so precious, and so important laying around for others to see. We always believe it or not thought it was just a story about the golden one, and I always assumed she would be a wolf and not an outsider from another world! And I swear to you that, I didn't think it was you till we got here. When certain things happened..."

"I know, its fine." She yawned trying to hide her tiredness with a stifle, so that he couldn`t see her tiredness. She knew he liked to fuss over her, he thought she was a weak female when she was a strong and independent woman!

He looked stern like she had expected.

"You need to go to sleep now. Let's go to bed soon, times moving on and we had a long travel to get here, Hope. And we have a long travel ahead I`m guessing, to get to grandmothers!"

She agreed for she was whacked!

"Yes, ok then, but separate beds. I will leave the book locked away here in the library, and then get it tomorrow, when I am more alert after all." She grinned and winked cheekily through tired eyes.

He chuckled back at his mate who did not know it.

CHAPTER FIVE

They travelled back quickly to her gorgeous room, eager for their luxurious beds. She was they agreed, to return for the book in the morning before their trip for some answers. He did not like seeing his mate so tired and unsteady on her feet, and so very worn out by all that had occurred. He wanted her to feel refreshed and with it, like she so was usually.

And raring to go, hopefully she would feel better after. As he was leaning in and giving her a sweet cheeky kiss on the cheek goodnight and biding her fair well back to his room nearby, a shrilling alarm started blaring out loudly throughout the whole of the palace, making them both clutch their ears with their hands, to drown out the loud noise vibrating harshly through their eardrums. What was going on? Why were all these alarms going off and causing a din!

He looked up at feeling others approaching them with his wolf senses, and worryingly to him he could see that his parents were the ones rushing quickly down the long corridor towards them both, looking more than stressed out and adjusting their clothing as though they had just thrown them on in their haste, to see what was happening in the perimeter.

It must be serious as they hadn`t even had time to take warriors with them like usual!

"What`s going on mother, father? What`s wrong, what`s going on?" Clay asked them worried. They looked really tired like they could keel over at any second, and they seemed fear-full about what was occurring from outside. It must be tiring being in charge of everyone and everything, Hope thought.

Clay knew however that good as they both were at being the current king and queen, and also the one true Alpha and Luna, that their time at reigning over them all was nearly at a natural end. Because they had been doing it for years upon years, and it was all he could remember since he was a young wolf boy, and it was soon time for them to pass the reign on.

To him.

Someone who was younger, fitter and who was also a fresh pair of eyes, and who could make fresh decisions. For things needed changing soon. And his parents had nearly had enough of ruling, you could tell. They needed some years on Triumph to just enjoy their fated mate, and the silence as they aged together disgracefully.

"New alarms? I don't remember them ever blaring out this loud before. "The prince asked his folk's. They definitely weren't, from what Clay could remember from back before.

"Rogues."

His father said one word, bluntly to his son. "Yes, they are our new palace alarms. Since the abduction and since as I told you earlier, an Earthling who thankfully turned out to be one of the good ones crash landed, then we have gone and tightened security here somewhat. We were much too vulnerable back then; I can see that now. Anyway, we need to go check what is happening out there son like now." The current shifter king growled and gestured his head to the great outside, and then he threw his large crimson royal cloak off to the side off the long winding corridor, like he just didn't care where his clothes ended up.

Which his father truly didn't!

His father always nearly let his mate his queen take the lead as she was the more dominating of the two that was for sure. But when there was danger coming there straight for them then they fought together side by side, and he would stand in front of her when needed and take any attack that came her way. Protect her. Give up his life for her, the same as Clay would do for Hope.

Rogues though. That was bad news if it was them causing the widespread panic outside.

"Drats. Are you sure? If that is the case then my Hope, you will need to stay here in the palace, in your room or mine, where it is safest for you, for it could be a serious situation that is ongoing out there, we do not know what we are dealing with. I cannot risk you getting hurt."

Clay said this all whilst starting to take his clothing quickly off, and just keeping a pair of tight, short like black briefs on as he could transform in only underwear and back again, or else he would likely rip his clothing up into a million pieces.

He continued on scolding her in a manner where she felt like a naughty child, but she knew that he was just worried for her safety. "You must stay. It is unsafe for you to come with us." He glowered, standing there his huge bulk, domineering even though he was in merely a pair of shorts.

Hopes eyes nearly bulged out of her head, at the sight before her!

"But I..." She argued fruitlessly.

"I said, stay here." He hissed at Hope. His eyes flashed in warning in a way that she did not like, and his teeth elongated which made her gasp in surprise at the way his mouth changed, and shiver all over at once.

She stated her case.

"I wanna help you all. Please. I know I have no wolf to assist, but I can help in other ways that don't involve ripping things, with my teeth and claws." She begged as his parents who were ignoring her as she seemed to them to be irrelevant right at that moment, started removing their clothing too to morph into their other halves.

Their inner beasts.

Clay faced her head on his face half beast and half man. Claws appeared on his thick fingered hands. Fur was starting to wind down his body, a gorgeous shade of black and grey colours. A tail appeared on his chiselled buttocks.

He shook his head in disagreement.

"You can help us by not getting in the way here my Hope. Stay here you must, that is an order from the shifter prince, and lock the door firmly shut behind you, and you only ever open it for me and for me alone." He spat out.

And then before she could argue any more with him like she so gravely wanted to, his wolf finally broke through the surface like the magnificent beast it was.

He howled loudly in a warning to all that might get in his way that his large wolf and built-in killing machine was coming for them, and then there was a ripping and tearing sound as his human body left for just a while, and his wolf was now unleashed to come out to play and to defend. And to conquer...

His parents did the same as their son at the same time in sync with each other, like they had done these many times before together as one. Two black wolves and Clays grey and black one along for the ride, beside them.

A force to be reckoned with if she ever did see one. The rogues would have no chance against the three of them!

She had never seen him like that when so close up and personal. Wow! His wolf was simply beautiful to behold, but also rather terrifying for an outsider to observe, as she yet didn't know it so well personally! He stood there in all his wolf glory with gorgeous coarse dark shades of fur, bright yellow burning like sun eyes, and a startling, fanged mouth that could rip through even the toughest of flesh. Claws that could rip through skin and leave scars.

But she knew this beast before her even in his wild ways looking like an extremely large rapid dog, would never ever hurt her or inflict any pain on her. Ever.

"Be safe please. Promise me you will come back to me, Clay. I need you. Always." She whispered gently into the moon shined night and only to him, and she waved at his parents well their wolves as they pounded on all fours down the long corridor, heading in the direction of the outside of the palace. Clays wolf stared at her sharply with his round moon like startling pale-yellow eyes for a few tense seconds, and then to her surprise he came over and gently nuzzled her with his furry soft head and eyed her in silent non spoken warning. Warning her to stay there in her room like he had told her to, and not to venture out.

Then the next minute when she was just enjoying his wolfy closeness and strange scent next to her golden caramel skin, then he ran quickly off in the same direction as his parents had presumably both gone.

To the palace grounds.

His wolf to see and to witness was very large and very quick on its four feet, super-fast as lightening as it zoomed off on its furry sharp, clawed paws click clacking on the ground and he would most certainly catch his parents up in next to no time, and then some.

She was thinking about going after them to see if she could help in any way, but then she thought that wouldn't` she make things worse by doing that? Probably. And he had told her not to leave, and she didn't wanna anger him in any way.

She had seen him mad and in a crazy up and down mood, and it wasn't pretty.

Thankfully though as she shut the heavy thick door to with a tug and double locked it, and checked it was shut tight then the alarms quietened, but they still rung out but lightly sounded. So, she assumed that it was to let people know that the danger was still ongoing but less so. Or maybe they just toned down after a while? She would have to ask later!

"Blooming males, telling me orders like they are the blardy boss of me. Especially Clay jeez." She muttered under her breath although there was no one there to overhear, and then going over to the fridge with a rumbling stomach, to see what was in it.

Something good she hoped so, to take her mind of what was happening that she could hear so loudly going on outside, but that unfortunately she could not see with her own eyes

She really hadn`t liked the way that he had ordered her about just a few minutes ago, but then she could hardly say no to the adored wolf prince of this planet, could she? One who had been nothing but good to her since on them both meeting, and not especially in front of his parents who were the king and queen!

She didn't think from her expressions and mannerisms on arrival that his mother liked her so much, if at all. But she did not care particularly what the female thought of her, the only two who she cared about on this pacific planet was Clay and his son Ruddy. She hoped that he was also ok, too but she assumed he would be as his dad would ensure it before any other thing, that his son was safe, and so would his parents.

She didn't know how it worked, maybe even Ruddy`s wolf was joining the battle? She hope not for he was still so young and should be tucked up safely in bed, not out in the dangers off the warm night.

She found whilst rummaging through the fridge some strange gooey, meat like substance and some bread and veg, and she managed to concoct some kind of sandwich, and some weird fruit like drink, whilst sitting on the large comfy bed flaying her legs backwards and forwards.

Her stomach knotted nervously and flipped over and over.

And frightening for her she was hearing the sounds of what sounded like vicious fighting beginning to happen outside in the palace grounds, like the opposition had breached the security of the long, tall fences and the old fashioned but strong drawbridge, and that they were trying to get into the palace itself. It scared her inside so very much that they whoever they were, were possibly so close she had to admit, but she mused that she was in good hands with Clay and his family.

He would do almost anything to protect her.

Because he was humongous like a man of steel and seeing him in those magnificent tight well-fitting pants earlier, she knew what was in them would be too! She imagined how he would feel if she lowered her hand and let it linger there. Stop it! She scolded herself for thinking about his firm, large, thick privates and about copulating together whilst he was out there in apparent peril, whilst trying to save them all from the dangers lurking outside.

She decided to be naughty, and to go and see what Ruddy was doing. She couldn't stand the thought of him being all alone in his room scared, or to be there outside. He had been through enough of late. She unlocked the door leading to the corridor, her hands gently quaking with nerves, and to her great most relief found that she was all alone, and that there wasn't a rogue waiting to tear her apart!

She pottered with silent feet, over to Ruddy`s room and stood outside and put her ear cautiously to the door. And listened.

"Hello, who`s there?" A muffled voice called out in but a whisper, from behind the solid wooden door. He was ok, what a relief!

"Ruddy? Its only me, Hope." She said quietly in but a whisper.

"Daddy said I`m not allowed to open the door Hope, unless it is for him. Go back to your room now or he will be cross and shout at you!" The young boy scolded her gently from behind the thick door.

She laughed lightly at his usual cuteness. He was so darn cute; she could eat him!

She tried to explain briefly.

"Ok Ruddy I will do, I was just worried that you was all alone, or that you were out there in the thick of it! I care about you that`s all..."

"I know. You too. Always. Thank you Hope. Your silly as if I would be out there fighting!" He laughed at her from behind the safety of the door. Cheeky monkey, he was lucky the door was locked!

"I don't know, how you people work Ruds!" She said defensively.

"Ok, I`m now going back to my room before Clay gives me a telling off, come find me if you need anything, promise?"

"Promise." Said the sweet shifter prince boy softly in a sleepy manner then yawning. She smiled broadly although he couldn't see it, and tip toed silently back to her room that Clay had chosen which she loved, which wasn't far thankfully.

She knew that Clay would be cross at her for venturing out of her room when he said not to, but she didn't care. Ruddy mattered to her, and he obviously was his dads number one priority, as he so should be.

She got back to her room and sat down wearily on the bed.

She thought for a few moments about the day that had just gone. About the library and their gentle to and fro flirting. About the alarms, and the now occurring fight probably happening outside! She wondered who the captain earthling was? That had plagued her interest, as her best friend Lynette had fell in love with an earthling called Raymond. She missed her so. She wondered how her friend was doing?

She sighed.

To her surprise she started to feel rather sleepy all of a sudden and she started to drift off into a deep sleep, that she couldn't so fight as much as she tried to. She wanted to be awake for Clay, to make sure that he was ok.

When she came to however long later then to her surprise, she realised she must have fallen asleep, and she had by the sun shining through the window, slept all through the night!

As she looked out of her large bedroom window inside her room, she could see that The Triumph orange coloured sun was blaring out brightly in the sky, the startling but vibrant colour of her favourite fruit back home, and yet darker then the sun that was the sun of her own planet.

The alarms had thankfully to her relief stopped sounding out, and she could sense that the storm had finally passed into the calm of day.

She got up after doing some light stretching, and had a quick but enjoyable shower, whilst also feeling rather bad that she had slept all night rather than staying up to see how Clay had got on with the rogues. She hoped that he was all right, she truly did. She missed him.

But then to her fear but also her waving joy, a loud and urgent sounding knock at the door sounded while she was in the shower, causing her to have to get out of it in a hurry. So she quickly rushed to get dressed in what little that she could get away with opening the door like, and opened the door warily whilst wondering who it was on the other side. And hoping to god more than anything, that it was a specific someone. Someone who was tall, thick, big and black. The prince of not just this planet where she was stood on, but her throbbing, happy heart as well. He could rule her any day, especially in bed!

She was pleased. For It was him who she dreamed of at the door, the one who she dreamed about every night since she had met him. Clay, not caring as ever barged through with a single thick set shoulder, and on his handsome face was a very tired but almost proud, victorious grin. He looked positively happy and glowing, which was frightening after the events of just the night before.

"My Hope." He said to her breathing huskily with his startling, manly voice that sent shudders through her. His voice making her shiver impatiently and tingle, and then feel increasingly wet between the thighs all of a sudden.

She adored and wanted this male so bad!

He began looking at her with a simply adoring gaze, his yellow, strange pale eyes never left hers once they pulled her to him with a force, that you couldn't see but you could most certainly feel.

Goosebumps went up her toned arms, and the light feminine hairs at the back of her neck rose in anticipation.

He didn't wait for but an invitation, he wasn't that polite no, and he went ahead and barged his way through into the room where he wasn't even staying, and shut the door then locked it quickly behind himself. Locking them in together.

So, they were now alone, just the two of them in the stunning room, with an inviting bed laid behind them. Calling their name, urging them to strip naked and wanting their liquids all over it....

"Clay, what`s wrong?" She asked him worried now, then she went and squealed in shock as he neared her like she was his prey that he had in its narrowing sights, and then he wrapped his large, huge arms around her, drawing her near to him and put his lips to hers, kissing her hungrily like he hadn`t eaten anything in weeks.

And like she was his meal.

For he could live off of her, and just her entire being. And he would die a happy man.

She hesitated at first on his lips hungry approach to hers, wondering what had come over him right then, and if this was the right thing for them both to do, but then she decided that bugger it! That she didn't so care, and instead drew his thick, luscious lips into her own full ones.

She groaned.

Enjoying the delicious, sweet taste of him. Wow this was a turn up for the books! She had never expected this, this morning on waking! He tasted as good as he looked, which was he tasted darn fine!

He then beamed at her with wonderment on his face, like she was his queen of everything.

Which she most certainly was, she just wasn't aware of it yet!

"You taste delicious my one and only Hope. But then I never expected any less of you and that full mouth of yours. I was truth be told, so worried about you when I was out there, and you were in here. I truly was when the rogues struck from the outside..." He said clutching her still, with his tight grasp between hers where she felt warm and safe, like no harm could ever come to her whilst she was hidden away from the world in his manly but firm bulk.

She was like a warrior princess, and he was her shield.

"It was all for you! They came for you; I think they came for you! They want you, but you are not theirs to have!" He spat out angrily, his eyes blazing with the hidden madness at it. He was fearful. Crazed.

"But why?" She asked carefully not wanting to rile him up further.

"That I do not know for sure yet."

He wrung his hands together making them creak with the pressure loudly. He needed something to take the pain of his soul away, and inflicting his own pain on himself might help? Who knew for sure!

"Hey, its ok Clay, you don't know this for sure, do you? Maybe it as they heard that you were back...And look, I was worried about you too, and you never came back to say what was happening last night like I thought you would. But I listened and locked the door like you asked though don't be mad, but I checked on Ruddy, even though I wanted to ignore you with everything in my body and come with you. I stayed here. I wanted to fight by your side where I belong. But who came for me? Tell me who they were!" She asked rather urgently stuttering on.

Her on the go mind leaving the unexpected, but really nice kiss that he had just given to her with his own soul, blessed her with, and also but wondering who had come for her, and what did they want from her?

Nobody good by the sounds of it.

Did he mean the rogues from the previous night before? But why would they want her for? She was just a nobody, from a planet that wasn't even their own one. One that wasn't as developed, or technology privileged as their own. Where they often struggled with no electricity, warmth and food supplies. But she was here to stay, with Clay and his son, for how long she did not know. But she wouldn`t be driven off the planet by that Star female that had her sights on him or the rogues either, and not after that sweet kiss he had given her anyway!

"The rogues, it was the rogues well some of them anyway for unfortunately there are hundreds if not thousands of them I presume. But they have been dealt with." He sighed mentally drained from being awake most the night but unable to sleep until he had checked his son and his mate had listened and stayed where they were damn well told to!

Inside in the safety....

"Dealt with? How so?"

"Dealt with. Dealt with permanently." He repeated firmly his face grim, until she slowly got his hidden meaning from his words.

"You mean they were killed?" She pulled back from him scared now, her eyes bulging and wide, looking horrified. A sick feeling reached her gut at her unease.

No. That didn't have to be the way! Surely not, there must be another way!

As if Clay could read her thoughts like a mind reader he spoke, the truth but in a calm and kindly manner.

"There was no other way, Hope. I`m sorry that you feel unease at it, but I only had to do what had to be done. If I didn't do it, then the king and queen would have done so in my place. And my way of destroying them was quick and painless as possible, and their way would have been longer like they did in fact actually rightfully deserve it to be.

He shook his head crossly. He didn't like it either all the bloodshed or the needless killing of their species, it made him sick inside. But rogues were just outcasts for a reason, and he had tried and tried before he was abducted on multiple occasions, to bring them back into the fold. Well, the ones nearby that was, as there was too many of them spanned across the globe to connect with.

But it just hadn`t panned out. Some battles you won, and others you had no chance of and getting the rogues on side and obeying rules that were laid out for them was one of them.

"There must, there must have been another way. Surely there was another option, Clay?" She said wiping a tear back from her long-lashed eye. She didn't like thinking of the death of anyone good or bad, and her emotions of late had been all over the place. It wasn't surprising after all that she had been through of late.

"Hey look at me. Now!" He drawled whilst wiping a lone tear away from her tearful eyes. "Hope we have tried everything to sort them out, I promise you eternally my wolf-less one. But no matter how many times we have tried me and my folks, to get them to re-join us and to stay in order, they were having none of it. And they pushed and pushed us to see how far we would go, hurting others on the way, and to see what we would take from them and their behaviour. But enough is enough already! You are here now, and I would die for you and Ruddy! We have already lost my best friend in this world Char and made poor Ruddy motherless when he shouldn`t be! There will be no more innocents deaths while I am around!"

He growled and struggled to keep his beast from unleashing like it was ready to!

Hope nodded, trying to show some understanding.

"Come here." He ordered on seeing her slowly moving away from him, pulling away. Hesitating as his beast wanted out of him. She did as she was told, for she wouldn`t have it any other way. She moved forward slowly one step at a time whilst eyeing him. She decided to take the lead this time and to hell with the consequences! She wanted him. She needed him. She was hungry for him.

She wanted to taste him, all of him from his head to his other head.

She pressed her full luscious lips to his making the first move this time and kissed him slowly at first then it soon became a fast and desperate need for each other.

He groaned at the passion of it.

He finally spoke.

"I am not sure that this is rightfully a good idea, my Hope. But I want it like nothing else in the world, I can tell you. I want it so bad. I want you. Only you." He sighed and paused and pulled back from her delightfully small hands. He saw her look at him with unease, wondering why he forever was holding back from her, and teasing himself and then teasing her in the process.

But If only she really knew how much he wanted her, and how much he desired her. He wanted to consume her, to fill her up with his children until she could bear no more.

"Why?" She said looking down at the carpeted floor avoiding eye contact with the amazing wolf shifter prince, who was like a practising magician who had put a hypnotizing spell on her...

"Hope." He said softly in a whisper and pulled her face gently, so she was looking at him. And only him as she should. "As your prince while you are on this planet, and therefore I now command you to look at me. Now Hope. This instant. Look at me oh sweet one."

She did so at once, she was scared not to. She shook gently.

She should have been angry at him for being so bossy and dominant to her when she should be able to be her own woman, and her own person. But to her complete and utter shame it was turning her on all his ordering about.

She could imagine his wolf teeth clamping down sharply on her slender neck and marking her for his own one. Though she knew she wasn't his, not really, she wanted to be his if only for just a mere day. For he was not hers to have. Or so she was not aware he was anyway!

He sniffed her openly, at last giving the game away.

"I can smell your desire for me, Hope. It seems to me to smell amazing." He licked his lips wickedly, and his eyes now bulged. And something else was bulging, pressing against her, as she looked down it seemed to...

"You what!?" She gasped astonished and pushed her legs together now, clamped tightly shut. Feeling awkward at him, smelling her ever needing want and desire for him.

And her desire for only him. For she couldn't imagine laying with another.

They truth be told since meeting had always had a small flirt together here and there, but nothing that would warrant his change in attitude towards her on that present day.

He faced her face to face and gripped her wrists gently with his hands so not as to leave a mark.

He repeated it.

"I said I can smell your desire for me. It has happened on numerous occasions from you that were not aware that I knew, but oh I knew! And I bloody well enjoyed it. But my Hope. I am but a half wolf, so what exactly did you expect from me?" His eyes glinted wickedly.

Her eyes bulged in her shock and embarrassment, and she tried to calm her wetness in her secret fur lined area, but she tried to do herself proud and act more confident towards the wolf man then she felt right now.

"Hmm. Not fair. I wish I could smell yours." She shamefully confessed to him, with a sinful want.

She couldn't believe that he had known all along her secret desire for him, she wondered if he had liked it, or if he was upset with it?

"You do not need to smell it; you can see it for yourself. It is yours." He drawled at her huskily, showing her answer to that question! His sexy voice spoke out making her all hot and bothered without what he was saying added to it as well.

It was hers for today and he was too, but for how long? She gasped and looked down to where his eyes were looking now. She could see that he had a massive bulge sticking out of his pants that was barely being contained by them. It was blardy huge! No way in all her wildest dreams would that monster he kept in his pants, fit anywhere near her womanhood!

She would need a new one after that!

She was lean and toned like many of her species were, small, curved hips and a tight ass, and well compared to her he was simply huge, big and buffed like the majority of his people were.

He repeated himself.

"I said you can see it. It belongs to you. And only you this day." He took her trembling hand with his huge one, and guided it, held it against him so that she could feel its entire impressive thickness for herself, and it's marvellous throbbing, long length. Whoa! On contact with it he growled quietly, and his eyes rolled back at the thought of her touching him any further, and of her finally venturing inside his pants with her small but still feminine hand and imagining getting on her knees and eating him all up with her rough tongue and full lips.

Until his cock was hidden from view.

He was hard as a brick now, and that was only just the beginning. And he wanted her before the doubts started to creep in, and then so took control of the situation.

"We are doing this." He groaned his balls throbbing along with everything else. "I don't care that it is a very bad idea, I just want it so bad, I must!" He said groaning as she started kissing him hard again, tasting him with her lips fiercely. Then they progressed to touching each other all over exploring each other's hidden places, and enjoying each other's closeness, and then he dropped to his knees.

She gasped in surprise. He pulled her trousers off and pushed her knickers to the side and pushed her gently to lay down and take it. His tongue started its pleasant journey, from her thighs upwards.

And after a long while of him gobbling her up inside her panties with his large wolf like mouth making her shudder in pleasure and bliss like she had died and gone to heaven, he turned her round put her on her knees eagerly and waiting for him, and he was finally inside her where he and his cock belonged....

His wolf took her hard in Clay`s body, and he then to her surprise but also her joy he marked her...

After they had dozed lightly for a few hours worn out now, enjoying laying side by side asleep for the first time ever together, they woke up. She turned over in the bed and found out that he was staring at her while she slept safe and soundly.

"Um Creepy or what!" She laughed to him, feeling slightly awkward that only a few mere hours earlier they had been fucking each other hard in all sorts of wicked but oh so fulfilling ways, and on that very bed that they laid in. And then other places.

She wouldn't lie, she had enjoyed every minute of it, and she would never forget it for as long as she lived, and she rued and regretted the fact that it couldn't happen again as he wasn't her mate.

For he wasn't hers to keep though unfortunately.

He chuckled hard, his laughter ringing through the room, and making her beam inside for the happiest that she had been in many years. "Sorry, I just couldn't resist staring at the beauty in this bed." He preened.

"I will let you off this time. So, about what happened before our nap.... It was good well great, but..."

"Well, what about it?" He said pushing himself up on the bed with his elbows and eyeing her. And turning to her and waiting patiently well impatiently, for her answer to his own question.

"It was amazing Clay it truly was no lie, but it was wrong of us...You belong to another female, your mate, don't you? Or are you rejecting her because that`s not on me..." She couldn't do that to someone else.

Even a stranger.

He faced her now his eyes blazing like burning suns, and he traced a single finger gently down her face, feeling her soft, warm skin.

He sighed feeling conflicted. "I would never reject my mate!" He roared making her flinch. And he wouldn't.

"I know! And I would never ask that of you, I know it's not in your wolves nature to, but we shouldn`t have done it, when you actually belong with another female! It's not fair Clay, it's just not fair!" She cried out in alarm, fighting back the tears that wanted to pour out of her body, in a swimming river of tears.

He gulped nervously rather loudly.

"I cannot believe after the few months that we have spent side by side, in each other's company barely apart from each other's side, that you still considering how clever you most definitely are, have not figured it out by now." He said cryptically again.

"Figured what out?" She glowered at him. Did he think she was stupid or something?

"The truth." He said in a rasp.

"About?" She asked the cryptic shifter wolf man.

He took a swift pause.

Was this it? Was this the right time for him to actually tell her the shocking and weird truth? Tell her who she was to him...But he was not a so patient man, and he could not wait another minute longer to, when she was so hurt that she thought he had another, so even if it was the stupidest thing that he had ever done in his thirty or so years, he went and told her.

He told her the truth of who she really was to him. And who she belonged with. With him, just him.

"You are...." He struggled to say the right words right then. For once the words were out and spoken with all honesty, then there would be no taking them back at all...

"I`m what?"

"You are my fated mate, Hope. It is you; it has always only ever been you. And I thought that you knew that too. How could you not know that I live for you? I would die for you. I only breath because of you and my son!"

She gasped and felt rather faint by the news of it. Her head spun. Wow! She was happy she really was, but wow, was it really true what he had told her? ...

She had of course wondered before this moment many times and hoped to god that she actually was his mate, and his alone. She had thought that maybe there was a chance, by his clues of his loving and caring words, and his simple yet gentle actions. And about how protective he was with her at times, when he did not need to be. And from the way that he so desperately wanted her to come back with him to the planet Triumph, with him. As if he couldn't bear to let her go for even a second, like it hurt him to.

But he had never told her the honest truth, so she had been forced to believe otherwise, until he was brave enough to.

Was she dreaming? It was like a fairy tale to her, but still right now it was a lot to have to take in. For he was after all, the wolf shifter prince and one day he would be the planets- Alpha, and their only rightful king. So, if she was his mate after all, then that would make her the future queen of them all! Oh crumbs...

She tried to respond but found it hard. She was shaking with happiness, shock and also anger she supposed.

"I.... I did suspect it was me but... I didn't want to get my hopes up Clay, in case I was wrong. So, I buried my head in the sand I guess." She shrugged feeling overwhelmed by all the emotions hitting her. It was too much.

"I am sorry, I truly am my little mate. You must know that I wouldn`t of slept with you, if my mate was else where! Never! We will go on our journey to grandmother`s as soon as, to see if she knows what is going on with the changing hair colour and all the crazy ass glowing. And to see if you are the one from the prophecy, or if there is another reason though highly unlikely for your change in appearance. But I think we find that you are the one. Is that ok with you? And when we so return here, and finally know what`s what, then I will shout from the rooftops to all and sundry that you are...That you are all mine." He pulled his head back and let out a celebratory howl that rang through the palace.

For there would be no more hiding things from now.

And with that he dragged his giggling, squealing, beautiful beyond anything, mate back to bed. where he eagerly marked her again, this time it would be a permanent mark. And now with her mark on her neck as they made love into the glorious morning light, and he took her as just himself a mere male and not as his wolf then she was at long last truly his....

The next day with a large, silky and glamorous scarf covering her neck like a hippy, sophisticated grandma, so as her mates mate mark was not to be noticed by any others in the city, as they wanted to keep their newly found mate hood on the down low from others, Clay and his Hope, headed off at last on their trip to see his grandmother.

The knowledgeable one she was. Having Packed only the bare essentials for the long and unknown journey ahead, the less they had to carry between themselves the better. He if he had had his way would have left with her in just their underwear, but then his eyes grew dark and the thought of another male seeing his one in barely nothing.

He hadn't been to see his grandmother in a very long time he regretted to say, possibly years and she had never come back for a visit at all to the main city since on retiring to the countryside. He felt like a bad grandson yes, he did, but then she had decided for reasons unknown to others to move away from those closest to her, and not even somewhere that was very close at that. But miles away...

For some reason she wanted out of there. She wanted to be free like a bird, like the rogues were, but without the whole being outcast like she was nothing part of it.

As she was so far apart then Clay said the pack link wouldn`t work well if at all and he was right for he had tried to get a hold of her, and she wasn't even on the telephone! So, fingers crossed that she would be where they so expected her to be. And that she was safe and well, and not in any danger.

Hope heaved a small bag behind her and had one firmly on her back with all the basics that she would need, whilst Clay with his large muscled arms, held one large one on his back like a pro and one small one in each arm.

"I hope that we have got everything that we will need. Are you sure we shouldn`t take a jetter?" She teased him lightly, knowing his hatred now for that sort of transport.

"No." Definitely not.

"Or you could go alone?" She eyed him and winked cheekily. Maybe the truth was not worth knowing at all, and besides they had each other now and would deal with whatever come their way together.

She just couldn't believe that all her fears and stresses had been for merely nothing, as it had turned out that they did actually belong together after all! She was blessed to have someone as fierce and powerful as Clay she truly was, though more than a little mad at him for keeping her in suspense all this time, and he had known all along!

As she was not a wolf then she hadn`t felt the mate bond pulling from inside like he would. It all made sense now and she if she had studied harder, she could have seen the big, blaring clues that were there in front of her face all along!

But now that he had marked her, she felt some strange and overwhelming pull to him like an invisible string was held there in place, that meant that they would always be able to seek the other one out, to connect with them wherever they may be. Whenever they so wanted. And he would look after her, that she was truly sure of without no doubts or hesitations. Take care of her, treat her like a princess forever on.

She had decided to bury her head in the sand and try not to think about the future though.

One where she was the queen of the whole fucking planet, ruling fairly but firmly by his side letting him make most of the decisions as he was destined to, and she guessed it that so was she in a way. She asked herself if she had no wolf, would she still be his wolves and his peoples

Luna? She must be surely! But she wasn't sure of the logistics of it all, as this had apparently never happened before.

She had decided that she would let Clay take that worry off of her lean shoulders for a time.

For he had had much longer to think of these things then she had.

She thought back to the night before, of their gentle but yet so perfect love making, and their not so gentle fucking afterwards that made her sore inside and out, but it was oh so worthwhile.... It had been over well a year for her since she had last actually done the deed, but even though it had been good with her last partner, no great in fact, it had been nothing like it had done with Clay.

As they were destiny's one and only. And they would have fun exploring more from now on. He was an animal after all!

"No, my Hope!" He growled at her gently on hearing that she would maybe stay at the palace and not come with and saying that he would have to make the journey alone, without her in place at his side. And his eyes flashed wildly without his control. Strangely hers flashed back in sync with his too.

"I was joking Clay, jeez."

He should have known! He loved it so fucking much! And her until the end of time.

"Your eyes Hope, they keep flashing yellow when mine do!" He said softly to her and cupping her chin so that her gaze met his again. His nerves dancing in his chest at the whole journey ahead of them. Was she as on edge as he felt right now?

"Are they?" She said teasingly. "Obviously she didn't have a mirror handy, but she could feel her eyes like they were doing stunts and acrobats, in her head. It would take a lot of getting used to this response to the mate bond.

Suddenly Clays eyes glazed over, and he went eerily silent in his concentration. She nudged him and called his name a few times, but he didn't respond. He had spaced out in his own zone and there was no bringing him back...

She was worried for but a moment but then...

Oh! It finally twigged what was going on! She remembered that he had said that when he spoke, or got spoken to by the pack link, that his eyes would glaze over and if he went in deep, he could zone out!

His eyes thankfully returned to normal then, and he frowned as though what he had been told wasn't good news.

"Clay?" She wrapped her arms tightly around him. The tingle returned.

"The book, the prophecy one, my father went into the library for reasons that I am not aware of why, and that pacific book is missing? Do you know where it is Hope. I really hope that you do, or someone`s taken it..."

"Oh. No, no I didn't, I was planning to return at some point to take it, to borrow it, but then the attack happened, and I didn't get a chance..."

He squirmed in her arms, and he growled and snarled.

"Of course, it makes sense now! I thought that they were coming for you because of who you are to me, but they weren't were they? They were coming for the blooming prophecy book!"

"And I was just a diversion..." It all made sense now.

"Exactly! I wonder if they are thinking the same as me, that you are the golden one from the prophecy? And if so then this whole and entire mission to my grandmothers has gone from a fun, finding out answers together trip to a dangerous one indeed....

"I wonder why they want it?" She asked him. "We need to hurry with our trip to your grandmothers, don't you think so? I think Clay that you don't really need three bags love do you!" She tried to laugh but the sound stuck in her throat. He felt the same way.

"I agree. Wait here at the gate near those guards." He pointed and went over and talked to the warriors. He then called out, "I am putting this away and I will be back, ok. Also, I have forgotten something of importance!"

"Your brain?" She rolled her eyes.

He just looked at her and raised a brow, then left quick as a flash.

She sat down on the soft, slightly dry grass outside the palace and plonked her bags down beside her. It needed to rain here soon for it always seemed so hot and humid.

"Oh, it's you." A voice called out behind her. She turned her head. Oh no! For behind her with her usual sneering look on her face was the betas daughter Star. Edging more and more uncomfortably closer.

"Yep, its me." She shrugged. Hoping the warrior bitch with a grudge for her would leave soon, for she was not wanted here by her. She left a bad taste in her mouth.

Star stormed over to Hope, ignoring the warning looks that the guards at the gate gave her.

The warrior snapped. "You know, I hope you get the answers that that witch grandmother of his has, and then take your answers and clear off back to where you came from!" She hissed in built up frustration.

"Don`t call his grandmother that!" Hope said angrily.

"Why, are you one too? Makes sense with all the weird stuff that`s been happening here ever since you appeared, what with the freakish glowing and hair, and the rogue attack! So, did you arrange the rogues, and did you kill his arranged mate too? Is that why you are here. To invade like the other aliens tried to?" Star snarled angrily, her eyes changing dangerously, which was quite scary considering that she had no wolf herself to help her and was currently being threatened by one.

Wow she is unhinged, Hope thought feeling slight panic and eyeing the guards hoping they would step in. Nope.

On the inside she was screaming, but on the outside Hope tried to remain calm. "No, no I didn't of course not. How could I plan an attack when I have only just got here, and his arranged mate that poor boy's mother, was attacked presumed killed in front of them! So Just go away! Leave us alone!" She screamed and the warriors tensed, and one remained while the other ran off, probably to get Clay urgently to come.

And before she could say owt more to the fuming and foaming at the mouth spitting female warrior, Star grabbed her scarf off of her neck with a yank and gasped at the large obvious mate mark on Hopes neck. Star then to her surprise growled, her fangs began coursing in, and before Hope could even blink to her horror, Star ripped her dress off until she was just in her underwear and turned into her dark furred fierce wolf.

A large black wolf, not as large as Clay`s no. But still intimidating to be threatened by all the same, when you had no wolf of your own. And the guards were beyond useless!

But then.

"Stand down Star, the warrior shouted out to her and creeping slowly and carefully over, but she wasn`t having any of it no, and she instead neared closer to Hope, who at that moment was trying not to shake in fear and was looking for the fierce wolf straight on.

The warrior shouted out and transformed into his wolf. Star came over to him and it was wolf on wolf, in a vicious battle. She knocked him to the side though knocking him out, out as though it was easy and nothing at all. For she was one of the royals strongest warriors...

Until it was just Star and Hope again.

"Come on then!" Hope shouted at the female snarling threateningly wolf either stupidly or bravely. Star neared her now, until she was at her feet waiting to find the right moment to pounce. To rip her to shreds!

Hope`s people could give an electric shock or a small burn with their hands in self-defence, but it hadn't worked on the Hazguard`s with their rough and thick like leather skin. Would it even work on a wolf? She had never felt the need to try it and she hadn`t used her powers in a long while.

When Stars wolf got right up to her Hope shocked her with everything that she had. Star winced at that, so it had obviously hurt her, but had it been enough to stop her from ripping Hope into a number of pieces with her sharp teeth? No, she didn't think that it had! Star carried on towards her and went to try to attack so this time Hope used her burn moves. Star screamed as the small burn hit her under fur. She snarled her fangs snapping like a crocodile in agony, and before she could defend herself, she went and bit Hope on the arm making her cry out in pain. Oh boy was she mad at her now! It still hadn`t been enough though, it was only meant to stun an attacker so as to get away not to hurt one badly. Hope didn't wanna feel those teeth again though! Gosh it hurt...

Suddenly she turned as she heard Clay over the draw bridge with some warriors shouting out in the near distance, Oh thank god, her hero! She could have cried with relief on seeing her man. Her protector.

He shouted at Star to stop what she was doing right now, his orders But her eyes lowered dismissively, she ignored him, and she acted as though she couldn't hear his orders at all. Her eyes glazed over, and Clay was obviously talking to her through the mind link as his glazed over too and he stood still on the spot.

Then Star thankfully turned back into her Triumphian female person form, not caring at all that she was standing there, in just shorts black briefs and a sexy like bra with most of her dark skin for all to see on display. She was a thing of beauty but what a monster she truly was!

Clay looked at Hope, at her neck where her mark stood from her scarf being brutally ripped off. Then he looked at her arm bleeding with a bite mark on it.

And he roared loudly with his wolf like he was some mad deranged lion at Star and turned abruptly back into his Triumphian male form. He slowly and surely approached Star, who by now looked a quivering wreck when she saw his fuming beyond measure face, and she realised what she had done, in her jealous madness to Hope.

She had pissed off the prince. One of the strongest shifters on the planet.

Hope gasped as Clay leaned over into Stars ear, and he spoke just one sentence to her that all nearby could hear.

"I am going to kill you Star."

The warrior female at that gasped, clearly afraid of his looming threat. Wondering, would he?

And before anyone around them could react or try to stop him as though she had done wrong her death would cause uproar, he turned into his precious and most powerful wolf who was forever there for him inside him, and he did to Star what he had said he would.

He killed her. And he fucking enjoyed it.

And blood and guts lined the land as the others looked on...

CHAPTER SIX.

Well after that turn of events the shit well and truly hit the fan on the planet of Triumph. Star turned into her wolf form as quickly as she possibly could when Clay lunged for her, to try in any way to defend herself, against the angry, looking out for blood and vengeance wolf prince. And also failing as everyone knew that she would, rather miserably in the process.

But she had had no chance anyway against Clay`s, all domineering, powerful wolf one of the strongest around. Who was now on a blood thirsty rampage after seeing his mate injured by another`s hands, and she only really had herself to blame for the way that she had finally met her early and unnecessary death.

It could have been prevented if she had kept her jealousy firmly to herself.

As not forgetting the fact that wolf shifters were always protective of their mates either arranged or fated ones, especially the males. And Clay was an alpha by his blood so his mate feelings towards Hope, would have been even more the stronger and clearer than others in their circles were.

And Star going as far as to attack and threaten to kill a non-shifter although it had never happened before, due to there obviously not being any non-shifter people on the planet until Hope had bravely appeared, was a disgusting form of practise even for her! Those that had just witnessed it, could not believe with their eyes what they were seeing at that moment!

To attack a person whilst in wolf form, and someone that couldn't even defend themselves at all in any way from the wolves attack, from their sharp pointed teeth, their long piercing crippling claws and overall, bulky physical strength, and to try to have a fair fight with them was just awful.

And Impossible.

A normal non shifter would have had no chance to escape the wolves wrath when it went for them in a rage!

Except lucky for Hope, she wasn't a normal non shifter woman by any means. Oh, no.

Star hadn`t been aware, not many people were, about Hope`s electric shock and burn powers that all her people were blessed with, which although not that strong in power had managed to prevent any further damage from Star to her body. But if Clay hadn`t appeared much to Hopes relief, then Star would have almost certainly of killed her, and not gave a shit about it either.

The signs had been there from the beginning for all to see, and Clay had warned his parents time and time again about the betas daughter behaviour before that dreadful moment, that it was unacceptable all the rumours and stories that she spread, the way that she nearly caused a civil war just from all her endless mindless gossiping and telling the wrong people things, and she had the males in a spin with her flirtatious teasing, when she only had eyes for one male.

One who wasn't hers to have.

And it had needed knocking on the head which is what would have happened if he was king, then there would be no more nonsense from those who liked to push their luck like Star, who wished to instead of acting like a loyal and faithful member of the pack, tried to push him in response to him rejecting her. She thought for some sad reason that it might make him want her. He could barf.

He knew that he shouldn`t have slept with her in the first place, he should have been stronger with his impulses, but she had been under no false pre tenses anyway that she was going to be any more to him than just a mere bed warmer.

She would have made a cold and rotten queen.

And he had known as soon as he arrived back, that she would have been giving him trouble and grief. The moment that she knew of Hopes arrival in the main shifter city, and when she knew of poor Charmain`s tragic death at the hands of the blue aliens, and when she discovered that Clay didn't have an arranged mate anymore.

She had seen him as wrongly hers for the taking. Until Hope had put the spanner in the works that was!

Star had gone feral or was on the verge of it anyway when she had attacked without thinking of the consequences. Her wolf inside her wanted Clays so badly as Star did, that in the end, that the only way out for her was meeting her death head on. The mind link and his order to stop had stopped working and she wouldn't submit under any circumstances, so there wasn't much he could do but to end her life.

There was no other way. She would have been a risk to the pack from then on in.

No one wanted to have to put down a pack member but sometimes that was the only way that it could be unfortunately...

So, in the end it was either Stars death or Hopes and then following that his own, as he in the event of his fated mates death, would have burnt the whole palace to the ground without a pause and gone feral himself, if anything befell on his precious fated one.

His one and only, forever and always. His Hope. And him, her wolf.

Beta Davidson had been called out to the area at once as soon as the fight had started, and he had come straight over to the palace gates which had taken longer than expected, where the scene of the crime was currently busy in clean up.

Not a pleasant sight.

He had come over after getting a panicked call that Star from was ignoring royal orders, to find when he got to the location that he was given, the wolf shifter prince covered from head to toe in his own daughter blood and insides going beyond crazy, as Hope stood shaking there with an obvious, injured wolf bitten arm, whilst trying not to throw up and doing endless gagging at the sight before her, and also trying not to feel bad of her mate Clay, as he was only doing what any male wolf most certainly would have done she had guessed.

His parents had not been far behind him when he had come running to save her from Star, and they themselves had done nothing to stop the attack, they knew as soon as they saw Clays face meet Hopes that he was about to lose his rag wolf style. For it was their sons decision to punish Star in the way that he had, and his alone. For even if she had been imprisoned, she would have forever been a risk to Hope, and Clay couldn't sleep easy at night knowing that his mate was at risk.

He couldn't bear it.

For yes Star might have been the second in charges daughter, the kings closest companion after his wife's, daughter, but she had to be made responsible for her actions that day.

Cos someone had to.

Clays mother Petal, who had been always abrupt and different with her since she had arrived on the planet Triumph, surprisingly had put a warm, loving arm around Hope and comforted her and reassured her in a loving and maternal way and had turned her weeping head away when the female shifters wolf guts started flying across their way!

For his mother the queen, was used to witnessing or being involved in rather gruesome sights in her lifetime, whereas Hope was not at all accustomed to it. This was all new to her, and she wasn't sure that she liked it! She wanted everyone to just get along like they should do!

Hope hadn`t wanted Star to die for attacking her, no of course not, and she wouldn`t of wished a mauling death on anyone. Even her greatest enemy, but she should have been imprisoned in her view for what she had done.

For she had made her choice, hadn`t she? She had seen the oblivious Clay leave to go back to the palace for things they had forgotten and had then taken that moment to try to destroy Hope.

Her one and only obstacle to what she believed was Clay`s heart.

Beta Davidson had more than lost his cool, as any father in that situation would have. On seeing his daughter there in that way. A cold, mangled mess that didn't resemble a wolf much now. He had then to everyone`s shock, challenged the king to fight to the death for the position as alpha.

Gasps could be heard all around. It had been a long while since the king had been challenged for his position.

Davidson yelled and pointed angrily.

"He killed my daughter, so now I will kill you, then your mate and also your evil deranged son, which Is the death that I will enjoy the most! I take no pleasure in killing my oldest friend right now, but he killed our beloved child. Our Star, so you must pay for it dear friend. Or I will die trying to..."

There was a pause.

The king as old as he was getting, and he wasn't as young or fit as he was hesitated. Plus, this man as upset as he was, and considering what he had just uttered, was his closest and most loyal friend of many years. But he now had to protect his family in the way that Clay had just had to.

Needs must.

The king remained conflicted you could tell. But then he nodded his head in agreement. For he could not appear weak, even if the thought of fighting his friend left him secretly shaken.

"Ok. But I will remain king after this fight, and then we will be needing a new beta, for the current one won't be able to breath!" And he snarled as they both transformed into their wolves in a hurry. For time was ticking.

The alpha and the beta stood head-to-head.

The Beta was simply huge, an imposing and intimidating mean looking, grey wolf, but the king was way bigger then he was, more impressive by nature, and he had obviously been in way more fights with his bulky stature in his time of reigning over them all!

The beta Davidson himself was no spring chicken either no, and he and then his wife who intervened after the fight, all met their death that very day at the hands of the royals, well their clawed paws. And the three of them the past beta family, laid there in a heap, lifeless next to their shameful daughter.

A sign for anyone who wanted to challenge either Clay or his father, the king, or to threaten their families, that this sight would be the outcome from it.

The king looked around and shook his head at the scene. He sighed then spoke.

"When you get back from your venture to my mothers, then we will have to call an urgent meeting son to discuss how we shall move forward from now on." the king said as he waved the others surrounding them off, so they could talk in private.

Everyone else left until it was only the king, the queen, Clay and Hope left standing outside, where the incident had occurred.

The bodies or what was left of them anyway, had been taken away as soon as they could get away with for burial, by any family that wanted to possibly claim them. Which was admittedly unlikely, given the shame that the corpses now carried from Stars own actions and from their challenges afterwards.

It wouldn't be done by the royals that was for sure, they wouldn't have anything to do with it, funding or otherwise like they normally did for close companions passings! But they had to tread carefully there, for the death of Star and then her parents, could cause the civil war that she had nearly caused before her death!

People had been obviously horrified by what had happened at the palace, some had come over to gather, but yet no one came to stand up to the beta and his family, because most agreed with Clays actions thankfully. He didn't want to get on the wrong side of the people, before he became the king. And before Hope became his own and only fated Triumphian queen...

"I believe that that, would be a good idea your highness." Agreed Clay respectably lowering his head to his worn out from the fight father. He nodded his head in his agreement.

Hope was still stunned though from the fight and the violence that she had witnessed and was still in some silent distress after the very recent events which had happened because of her. She couldn't get the image of Clays wolf tearing the stirring female apart with ease, the grotesque sight of gore and of blood, and the female dying because of her.

The queen came over to Hope, in a few elegant long steps, her black crowned hair perfectly held in place as always, and her jewelled gown glinting in the sunlight catching the sparkles of the jewels embedded within it. She wanted to talk to Hope alone, while Clay and his father were busy discussing a few things that needed airing before the two of them left on their way.

"I just wanted to say to you that I am truly sorry for giving you the cold shoulder before Hope, and for not welcoming you with open arms before. I just didn't realise how much you meant to Clay, and I didn't realise that he would mark you for his own! And I also didn't realise how much Star was going to try to get in between you both, and to hurt you, even after being rejected by him on a fair few occasion. I thought that they might have been a good match for each other before, considering she was the betas daughter, and we were all so close like family." She looked down sadly.

"But I am not too fearless to admit that I now realise that she was simply bad to the bone, and not at all right for my Clay. I have known her all of her life, and I was close as could be to her parents, but in the end, it was the only outcome that there could possibly be in the end after what she did to you without any regards. And Char was like a daughter to me. I know how things were between them I am not stupid, but it will hurt for a very long time, her passing all of a sudden..."

"it's ok, I guess... And I never had the privilege to meet her but she from everything that I have heard about her seems like she was an amazing female. It's just all a lot to take in all this. I am not used to this happening to me. Much as I adore your son, we don't have any shifters where I am from..."

"Well, you must take all the time in the world to find your feet while you are here Hope. Though I hope for Clay`s sake, it is a permanent thing. Come lets go out of the way and let these two talks." She touched her arm gently and walked Hope out of the talking seriously males earshot.

Clay watched them both waltz of for a fleeting moment, and then continued his conversation. Side by side it was now noticeable how like his father, Clay was in both looks and kind nature.

Dread hit her chest and dropped to her stomach when the queen took her aside, that was in case her majesty's reassuring words were all just for show in front of her son and husband. She hoped not!

The queen surprised her though when she continued behaving herself though. "I myself was not born to lead others either Hope, I married into the throne Hope when I met my mate. He was just like Clay is, the wolf shifter prince and it was a complete surprise to end up mated to royalty when I first discovered who he was! And his mother being a witch was hard to take in at first much as myself and you probably! But my mate much as I love him, is so utterly peace loving and quiet, whereas I am obviously the more domineering out of us both, as you can probably tell! But quiet as he is, weak he is most certainly not. He is both physically and mentally extremely strong. You although I don't quite understand them much, have your powers, and you will find your own personal and unique strength over time also."

"Thank you, your majesty." Said Hope sincerely. She was glad that the queen seemed to have changed her tune with things.

The queen smiled politely, and then sighed. "So, about your powers?" She asked.

"It is just like a built-in self defence mechanism that all my people in my species have. I can give out a shock or a burn, never both at once and it is tiring. It if I am brutally honest, the trick does not get used much on my planet, as we only really use it in times of great need or attack. It does not always work though; it depend on the species. It seemed to help stop Star before from taking a chunk out of me, but my close friend Shane back home was nearly abducted by the Hazguard`s, and unfortunately his powers didn't work on them barely at all from what I could see. Their skin is thick and scaled in places though which I assume stops the shock and burn from working."

"Hmmm, interesting." The queen Petal said rubbing her chin, whilst thinking. "Well as long as you look after Clay and my grandson, then I will keep an eye out for you, and my mate will of course. But I think that you won't need our help in the end. I think you will do just fine."

"How come?" Hope asked cautiously.

"I just have a feeling. And I don't know but I have and feeling in my old bones that you are special. And you will make a good queen soon. Just be warned that I don't know why but your scent seems to smell off."

"I smell?" Asked Hope aghast.

"No dear!" The queen chuckled. As her son and fated one came over to join them. They had finished discussing the ins and outs of various things. "I meant your scents off, not that you smell bad!"

"Her scent?" Said Clay catching the tail end of the conversation between his mother and mate. He had a smile on his face, his eyes twinkling happily at seeing the two females in his life getting along finally. His mother was a glorious woman obviously, she was of course related to him, so it was in her blood! And he knew she had her reasons for her ignoring his mate before, but he was pleased that she had started to thaw out with her cool attitude towards his out worlder mate.

He knew that it had made her uncomfortable and maybe he should have stepped in to say something, but a lot had gone on in the short time that he had been back, and he had missed his parents so gravely much!

He didn't think that Hope would leave him now she knew the truth about being his fated mate, but he really didn't want anything to get in the way of keeping her there on the planet Triumph with him and forever by his side.

He sniffed. "That`s strange it does smell different. I wonder why..."

"Maybe because we are fated mates?" guessed Hope, trying not to get offended when his dad also took in a big sniff too causing Clay to occidentally let out a growl, at another male sniffing what was his even if it was his dad and he was mated to his mum!

Hope fidgeted on the spot and wondered what they meant by her scent having changed...

Suddenly out of the blue and taking her mind of feeling like she most possibly stunk of something really bad, a painful shooting cramp went through her abdomen, causing her to cry out in pain. She fell straight to her knees as it radiated downwards to her legs, gosh it hurt so bad! What was the reason behind it?

Clay saw her sudden discomfort at his eyes corner, and he immediately came rushing to her aid, and helped her to stand up and to lean on him.

"Hope, what`s wrong, my Bekuna flower?" He asked her concerned by her clutching onto her stomach in sheer agony and standing there sweating profusely. A wave of dizziness hit her making her feel faint also. She would have blushed at his sweet comment, which was unlike him, if she didn`t feel like currently something was going to tear out of her body at any given moment.

"I`m just feeling a bit funny Clay, for a moment, its fine honestly." She said faintly.

Luckily as Clay gripped her in his worry of her, openly staring at her like she might grow two heads and explode, the agonising pain seemed to pass through her and then thankfully for her it disappeared into the hidden unknown.

She shakily composed herself and tried to act like it hadn`t bothered her at all, when it had so.

The king looked like for once, he wanted to say something. He muttered something quietly to his mate beside him, and she nodded sullenly.

"I think it might be best if you both delayed your journey?" The king finally spoke up. And the queen murmured her agreement, and moved to stand closer to him like they drew each other in.

She would stand by her mates side until their time was done and dusted.

Hope shook her head, not wanting a fuss. "No, no its fine now honestly I promise you, I would say so otherwise, and I would really like for us to get a move on with our journey soon, to see your mother who I have heard so much about, your highness."

He didn`t seem to agree though.

"I insist that you both stay at the palace for the time being, and put your venture on hold, until young Hope is up to it." The king said concerned at Hopes paling withdrawn face that she was trying with little to no success, to hide. And whilst secretly thinking that the two of them going on their adventure to visit his mother right then, the planets great and knowledgeable witch, would be a really, really bad idea.

For in the kings opinion, Clay would be much too worried about his mate to be on the ball with things to even be looking out for any danger in the great unknown. For once they left the city, which would where the risk of rogues and other creatures would increase. and Hope could on the way get a repeat of her pain, and then they both would be stuck. Alone.

Clay eyed his dad with his piercing yellow, stern eyes, not happy at his father's interference in matters that he thought he had the rights to.

Uh oh, the alpha and future alpha appeared to be bumping heads on the subject and going head-to-head!

Clay eyes grew wide at his father's remark. "Is that an order, your highness or are we free to go on our trip as we please, like my mate so wants to? "Clay said to him crossly, in a manner that only he could get away with talking to their rightful king like.

And grabbing his mates clammy hand and squeezing it tightly with his own. Feeling unknown emotions run through him at the speed of light, as yes, he had loved before, but he had never actually been in love with someone.

His father frowned all of a sudden and quietly studied them like they were a magazine, lost in his own thoughts.

The stressed-out king ran his dark fingers through his black like the night greying hair, and his wolf shone through, just a glimpse but he was there, and he was getting more and more pissed.

The queen was right when she said that her husband was stronger than some shifters gave him credit for. But also, in a way if the two of them hadn`t have gotten married and been fated mates, then he might have struggled to keep his position as alpha and as king. For the king wasn't as alpha like material as his son so blatantly was, or his queen was for that matter. But he was still a good man, with a good soul, and he had tried with everything in his power to improve the packs in the best way that he possibly could...

The alpha stood his ground. He stood tall and wide, to let his arrogant, slightly frustrating son knew that yes, he prince of the shifters, but the king was still the boss- for now...

The planets ruler shook his head.

"I could Clay if I wanted to if I was being stubborn... But I know how much it means to Hope to find some answers to all this mystery circulating. But I do insist that you keep the pack mind link open for me and your mother, and that you take one of the newer one phones with you and a memory bank. Deal?

"Deal." Clay shook his dads hand and smiled and him then pulled him in for a hug. Hope smiled at the pair. She wondered how her own parents were getting on back home without her, and she hoped that they hadn`t run into any trouble with the brutal, blue aliens?

They hadn`t if she was honest with herself been all that close of late, which she wished she could change and she had sprung her departure on them very last minute, which they hadn`t been happy with. But they were still her parents at the end of the day, she worshipped the ground that they both walked on, and she with all her heart, forever would.

Family was family after all.

She knew how much Clay loved his family also, especially his son and sister, and she hoped that one day she would be able to build a bond with them while she was there.

While she was there? That was a subject that she was trying not to think of for the moment. Being on her own planet, with her own people and her dear family vs being with Clay her mate, and his ones. Something would have to give eventually. Now she knew how her friend Lynette felt when she found love with the earthling Raymond and left as soon as she could for earth. Hope had not seen her in five long years and missed her friend greatly.

Five years... She didn't think that she could keep away from her beloved family and her friends for one year, let alone five! She needed to think carefully before she made a rash decision. And maybe, just maybe, on this journey to his grandmothers she could. And anyway, she still hadn`t let it sink in that she had a forever mate! Wow.

But she had no doubt in her mind that Clay was not someone that she was willing to give up. She had no wolf, which was right no but she could feel him, like he was actually her. They breathed the same air, and they both beat as one. Was it fate that brought him to her planet? Even if in the most horrible of circumstances by being imprisoned and taken from his home? It must have been, for what other explanation was there for the two of them meeting like that?

"I still think you should let the poor girl rest." Murmured the queen looking at her mate who was staying tight lipped now.

Hope who was stood there in a daze, spoke up out of the tense atmosphere. "I tell you what, how about we stay here one more night, I can rest and see how I feel and then we will go in the morning, after breakfast."

Clay looked at his mate like she was the sun. "Hope, if that is what you want."

"Come then." Said the queen holding out an arm for Hope and her mate held her other one. "Oh, and Clay bring the bags, and maybe tomorrow don't take as much eh. That`s if you don't want to take a jetter that is! She chuckled and winked at Hope.

"Oh, ha-ha!" Said the wolf shifter prince as he dragged all the bags back towards the palace.

Well in the end they didn't get to go on their travels across the country, the next day after all or the next, or even the next day after that! Because a freak storm materialised out of the blue, without notice and it wasn't on any weather forecast. Strangely, it had rained nonstop ever since they had decided to stay at the palace for just another night, and the air ever since had been nothing, but the loud pitter patter of rain drops, bright lightning flashes and noisy thunder clashing through the sky.

Which truth be told, was rather unusual for the planet, and apparently it was all over the world, not just the city that they were currently in! It was a planet that was very, very hot and it didn't usually rain much often, meaning that they had to collect the rainwater or use the rivers and lakes waters. But when it rained, by hell it so rained!

And this rain didn't seem to be wanting to stop any time soon, no, for the two new mates to continue on their way.

It was strangely as like something didn't want them to go out there at all...

Hope stood at Clays large, curtained bedroom window, staring out at the astonishing for her weather. She was in his room which she had due to all his nagging and insisting became Hope`s sole room also. He did not want to be kept from her another night, now she was his.

And the mate mark that lay bold and proud on Hopes neck and in which would be there for life like a welcome brand, and what they were going to keep hidden until they returned to the city, after their trip of discovery? Well, everyone and anyone knew about it now, and knew that it was there so it was pointless hiding it anymore! This was in part thanks to Star ripping her scarf off of her neck in her anger, and therefore others seeing it, and then gossip spread through the city, and some shifters didn't know when to shut up....

It was big news, of course it was. The prince and the soon to be shifter king and alpha had a mate. And shockingly she was not of their planet, but an out-worlder...

"I have never seen rain go on this bad or this long in all my days." Hope said to him, as Clay began pacing the room like an animal. His wolf inside him, did not like to be caged inside like this with no way of getting out to run wild and free. Soon he would have to if it carried on fuck the rain and go for a run in it. It wouldn`t be a pleasant experience no, but anything was better for the wolf and shifter, then being forced inside like being in a prison.

The beast needed to roam free and run through the forests.

Clay didn't say anything he just kept pacing.

"Clay, Clay? He didn't respond, it was like he was in a trance.

"Oi you." That snapped him out of it, he turned and looked at her frowning.

"Was you talking to me, my little cute princess?" He said coming out of his daze.

"Yes, I was. And anyway, I am not little, and I am not a princess! What is wrong with you, you know you can tell me anything?"

He sighed and looked at her with a painful expression. "One, you are rather little compared to me, and two you are a princess, and one day you will be queen of them all!" He growled, and his eyes shone bright yellow. She would never get used to seeing that, it was eerie to see. "And three my love, I am feeling trapped."

"By me?"

"Never!" He yelled out, a bit too loudly making her flinch and step back in surprise. He shook his head and came over to her. He pulled her into a tight embrace. "You will never trap me, but if you did, I would enjoy it plenty, especially if you trapped me with your tight, little pussy."

She gasped and a red colour appeared on her caramel skin. "Clay!"

He laughed at her obvious discomfort. He pulled her closer to his person and sniffed her welcoming scent that reminded him of his favourite flowers in the palace gardens.

The Bekuna. He would never forget the smell of her as long as he lived, he would follow its scent across the planet, just to get to her, and to stand by her side, where he so belonged. No, if anyone had done the trapping then it was him, and he knew it in spades. He knew that he could not push her, push his luck for she was of a different world and if he angered her, she may go back, he must tread gently...

And he thought panic reaching him and causing unease through his body and going into his wolf, that he would never ever get over losing her...

CHAPTER SEVEN

The rain went on for more days than they thought. But then the rain had just simply disappeared from existence into thin air, much like it had actually never actually been there at all. You could only tell that it had even rained due to the wet sodden grass surrounding the palace walls, and the patches of flooding encroaching on the land that had arisen from it.

Clay sat there fidgeting on his gorgeous large comfy sofa, like he had ants in his pants from being enclosed for so long. Which he had.

Hope looked over at him fidgeting in his seat for the millionth time.

"My wolf needs a run my Hope." He said being brutally honestly with her, like he could hear what she had said. "How about I take him for a nice run to let some steam off with him for a time, and then afterwards we can finally go on our way, on our trip, which is if nothing gets in the way with it again!" Clay smirked to his mate, who was currently busy pottering around the small kitchen area like she owned the place which she sort of now did, whilst trying to clumsily make them both something nice to eat, from the tall fridge freezer that he had in his much bigger room, then hers was.

She put his meal out in front of him with a clatter and laid out the cutlery and some napkins, as she knew how messy these males could be with their food! Especially him! It was hard for her to prepare the meat in the way it should be, as the food here was different then what she was used to back on her home world so she wasn't sure how long it needed to cook, but in fairness her making it had come from a place of love, and she had tried her best with it to make it look and taste nice for her new beau.

Tried to make it presentable and enjoyable for her, eek! Mate!

She was still getting her head around that vital piece of information! But she much as it scared the beseezus out of her, really wouldn`t want it any other way! The annoying but oh so dashing male who was now her own forever mate had entranced her from the first meeting and she felt like she was currently living in a fairy-tale.

She thought that was a good idea for him to go out. She knew he hated being cooped up.

"That sounds like a good idea sweetie." She replied to the hunky wolf shifter before her nodding her head in agreement and gave him a gentle but tender kiss on the lips. He tasted to her so good, she could frankly kiss him all day and all night, and not get bored!

When the rain had fell hard from the sky, when they were due to leave, like it was falling in buckets upon buckets, and like it never wanted to ever stop. Then they had made the most of being stuck inside and trapped inside alone together, and they had spent a few days treating it like they were on their honeymoon.

With constant fucking each other, talking, eating and then back round in a circle again. She felt a wave of heat between her legs at the thought of what had occurred between them both in the past few days. Memories that she would never forget or would ever want to. And ones that she would treasure for all of eternity. But it was no good her being shy about their adventurous copulating now, for Clay was a wolf shifter with a very high sex drive as was usual for a male shifter and that had been curbed for a long while, and so she definitely wasn't complaining about it when he wanted to rut with her multiple times of the day!

For how could she say no to that!

She had wondered to herself at times when times were quiet, if the wolves did the deed in their wolf form also as well as in shifter form. But she had been afraid to ask Clay in fear of looking like some deranged pervert with a secret animal fetish! She most certainly didn`t that was for sure, but she had a lot of questions about shifters that she still didn't know the answers to!

For she couldn't keep asking him stuff!

Little Ruddy in all the wet weather, had gone on to spend some alone time with his grandparents in their massive apartment as he had missed them both so very much in his time away from home, and they him. More than anything.

He sweetly, still popped in every evening at the same time for a few hours to eagerly see his father and also to hang out with Hope. Who he thought was cool as. So, the mates had had to time their frantic and energetic love making, so as not to clash with the expected time that the wolf boy would knock and appear at their door, jumping up and down, and wanting them to play with him for a while or entertain him somehow! He hated being stuck in as well.

His son normally came over after dinner he was like a little happy puppy dog who wanted cuddles and affections, and though he wasn't hers, Hope adored him so frightfully so!

They had to make sure they were finished exploring each other's hidden areas, as they didn't want to traumatise the poor thing on arrival, by him witnessing something that young eyes shouldn`t have to witness with his small innocent eyes!

Clay got on eating and stuck hungrily into his food much like he hadn`t eaten at all for a year, and then licked his thick lips as the meat hit the spot. It was just delicious he thought, and hope was learning! His wolf handily caught his own meat for his own consumption like most wolves did, not that he had told Hope this information of course! He wasn't sure that she would be thrilled by the needless killing and then eating, even though she herself wasn't vegetarian or vegan, and she did occasionally eat meat.

And last night to Clays delight, she had most certainly enjoyed eating his own meat very much that was for sure, that laid out for her large, thick and standing eager and proud between his firm thighs! It had had more action lately then the poor thing had ever had in its thirty years, but it didn't seem to mind or want to stop getting hard and ready for her any time soon!

He shuddered at the thought of it, of her wet and pleasing cunt, making it yet again grow hard in his pants with a firm twitch.

When he saw Hope watching him eating with curious eyes and licking his lips happily in his glee at the dripping meat and accompanying food, he looked at her with his own hunger blazing in his eyes, hunger for her and decided to put on a show for her with his eating his food, and licked his lips, and moaned naughtily for his mates enjoyment.

His eyes twinkled in his playful amusement when she started fidgeting awkwardly, and blushing and her sweet scent of arousal hit him hard and kept it hard.

She shuffled and glared at him like he was a bad man, for she knew exactly what he was doing to her! The blardy wind up merchant!

"This tastes good, you're a good cook." He said complimenting his horny mate for her culinary expertise. She hadn`t burnt it and he liked it hardly done.

"I did overcook it more than you like, I think. Sorry." She shrugged apologetically at him. He could cook it himself if he was that bothered, she wanted to impress him, but she wasn't his maid!

"No. It is good. You must never apologise to me, for its a fine piece of meat, tasty, and delicious just like you are." He growled softly.

"Did you just compare me to a piece of meat?" She glowered, putting her hands on her hips in mock outrage Ent at his passing comment.

He looked guilty. "Er, maybe..." He grinned cheekily at her.

But how could she ever get cross at him with his handsome beaming face, and he was far too sweet and silly and kind-hearted, to get mad at!

But then interrupting their playful banter, the door went, and she answered it to find his son surprisingly there. Early as.

"Oh Ruddy, it's you. You, ok? Your early sweetie."

"Yes, I just knew to come early today." He shrugged, and rubbed his dark cute curls that were wet, so he had obviously snuck out into the rain!

She said on seeing him at the door and inviting him in. "Come in then." He grinned at her then stuck his tongue out at his dad in a cheeky manner.

"Oh, you are both eating, yummy it making me hungry again! I`ve had mine though, Nana said I couldn't come here unless I ate it all...." He said, but his eyes lit up and he still hungrily stared at the couples nice smelling food. He was a young growing boy with a hungry appetite like most boys did, and he also had a growing wolf to contend with also, who demanded meat on the regular, and turned its nose up at rabbit food.

"Would you like some food Ruddy?" She asked him, as Clay watched the two, he loved the most, getting on lovely together as usual with a warm feeling in his soul.

The lad skipped over to her and her dishing up the food.

"Yes, please Hope. I just wanted to say bye before you both went on your travels, to see my great Nana. I have not met her ever as she moved away from here before I was born. Is she really a witch? Oohh exciting if she is!" Ruddy said throwing himself down on the large sofa opposite his father. The two of them near each other were like two peas in a pod, they looked so alike it was uncanny!

She looked inquisitively at the young male, her mates lovely, adorable son.

"How did you know we were going soon?" She asked him. "And I don't know much about your Nana, you will have to ask your father about her." She said looking pointedly at Clay, who acted suss as though he wasn't even aware of the conversation that was going on.

But she thought that she had an inkling why Ruddy knew.

He chomped down the food he was currently chewing on. "I don't know I just had a feeling in my bones. A strange feeling."

Hope went over to him and said.

"You know Ruddy, I think you have a bit of magic in you like your aunt Shelly, and your grandmother do." She playfully bopped him on the nose now and smiled at him lovingly now that he had wolfed down all his food like a good kid, a blatant pig like his father was! It hadn`t taken him long!

"I don't know maybe...Shelly does too? Is she a witch too?" The boy asked excitingly. He adored his hip aunt.

Clay butted in. He was defensive of his sister like brothers often were, and he was not keen on the term witch being thrown about!

"Not a witch no son, but she knows things that she shouldn`t possibly know. She knew that Hope would be important to me and Shane to her, and she said it is important that I become king. And she didn't mean it in just an egging me on sisterly way, she knows something that we don't." He said in all seriousness.

"Like when I knew to go to Hopes friend's house instead of anyone else`s, when I escaped from the beasts?"

"Exactly like that son. Exactly like that." Clay said ruffling his cute sons dark hair in a fatherly way.

"Can I come on a run with you pleaseeee? I won't get in the way daddy. And Hope can have her food in peace." He said pleading.

"How did you? Never mind... Yes, come on lets go get out of Hope`s hair." He gave Hope who blushed a quick kiss on the lips, and his son giggled and pulled an ew face when she squealed.

"Cool. Bye Hope. See you when you get back." The small boy pulled her into a comforting hug. He had grown more confidence since his wolf had turned up just a few months back, but it was a shame to see that his mother would never get to see it for herself. She would be, so, so proud.

"And you." She returned the hug to the waiting wolf boy.

Father and son both waved to her as they both hurriedly went out of the door together.

"I will be back to pick you up in a few hours, my sweet." Clay said on the way out with the boy. She nodded. He stopped in the doorway and looked over at her in challenge. "Oh, and Hope? Lock the door, and I command you do not let any male in this apartment, who is not related to me." The prince said with a warning tone to his words. His eyes shone out, and he looked like a wolf possessed!

What the! She would never understand him!

She was about to follow him down the long palace corridor, and to give the stubborn shifter a piece of her mind, but he had already gone.

"Just wait until you get back here!" She muttered crossly to herself now finally sitting down to eat, though she wasn't that hungry, for she was now alone in the room and could enjoy the peace, but she also had like a million and one thoughts running through her head.

She couldn't believe how stupid she had been all the while, all the time that he had been jealous and possessive of her so often and she hadn't had a clue how he had felt for her! Or that they were fated mates!

Stupid or what!

The time passed by quickly and she while her love was away, compacted their bags from before which were way too many into a smaller load. Yes, he liked others to know how big and strong and alpha like he was and relished caring all her bags, but in the end, they would just get in the way.

She had a quick clean-up of the apartment, and before she knew it, he was there at the door for her.

He chatted nonstop in his oh so sexy thick foreign accent, about how happy he was to have finally unleashed his inner wolf and had enjoyed joining his son on a final goodbye run.

She was enjoying listening to him that much that she even forgot to scold him for what he said before on leaving! His mood had perked up so much, just with one bout of exercise. It was plain for all to see, that all the shifters needed to be out and about in the wild or they became more and more depressed.

It was a goodbye run, for they did not know how long they would be away from the city in the end! Or back to each other.

On lugging the bags, though he carried the most, they were met by his parent and a large group of others who all to Hopes shock and surprise turned into their wolves one by one at the palace gates, and all sat at his feet and howled. His eyes shone out and he turned to Hope briefly and said. "It's a goodbye tradition."

And then before she could respond to him, he turned into his large black and silver wolf, and joined in all the loud in sync howling, and running around with the others for a good five minutes. Hope was awestruck.

And then he turned back into his normal form while the others stayed in their wolf form to watch them leave.

He hurriedly put his clothes on in a dash, although he did not need much clothing, what with the ever-eternal heat on their world, making him drip sweat down his firm pecks.

Hope was stunned, for she had never seen so many wolves together in one place at once in all her time. It just goes to show and remind her, that she was actually on the planet Triumph, rather than her own one....

And then after that, they left the marvellous, huge palace and started their journey into the great wide unknown. Well, it was all unknown to Hope anyway as a stranger to the planet, for Clay had been here, there and everywhere in all his time on Triumph, as a great and mighty shifter wolf prince. He had been born and raised a prince, and all he knew was his parents as king and queen.

He had travelled all over with his folk's and his sister while he was younger and growing up into who he was meant to be. And was then taught over the years to follow the peoples ways and shown what exactly would be expected of him when the time so came, for him to rule the nest.

So that he was ready, when the time came to take over from his father. Ready to rule them all.

So, Hope was excited about what she would see on the upcoming trip, but also extremely eager to reach their destination. He had never been on a trip with a lone female before admittedly, and not one that made him want to get his impressively tight-fitting loincloth out for show again and show her what she was missing underneath it!

And now after all the pack had left for home, and it was just the two of them for the next few days, possibly weeks or so. Walking through the glorious city together side by side like the mates that they were, Hope looking wide eyed at all the passing beauty of everything surrounding them, and gasping in wonder at the sights, and also sweetly holding hands with each other.

Tingling reaching each other's bodies at the skin touching. Craving it.

And enjoying starting their trip in to the wilderness alone together.

The animals that they passed by were like nothing that she had ever seen before in all her days. But many of the creatures that they saw kept well away from them on seeing the large, handsome dark-skinned male beside her, guarding his precious one with his life. From their fear...

The insects on her world were small and mainly harmless, whereas here they were often bigger than them! And Clay was well over six foot. She nearly had a heart attack on them accidentally bumping into a black and yellow, six-foot-tall bumble bee with a huge but deadly stinger on its backside. Clay explained to her whilst slowly steering his precious one away from it, that the stinger of the bee if the bee was provoked would kill you instantly for it was dripped In poison, and then the bee itself too would also die after its stinger became ripped off and left in its victim.

Sad times.

They passed by mysterious tree lined woods, various animals like nothing she could ever have imagined, grazing in the streams, nibbling at their catch of the day. She could hear the dragons that Clay had told her of, and that she had luckily seen previously with her own eyes, flying about in the distance.

But she knew disappointingly that it was unlikely that one would leave the safety of its nest again to come to see her.

Because according to Clay, it had never happened before.

"What is that?" She uttered on seeing something new in her side eye, that yet again caught her excited interest. Her mind leaving thoughts of fire breathing terrifying dragons and homing in on a new species before her.

For a petite beast trotted over. Much like the horses that Clay had shown her before at the palace, came towards her with round, watching curious eyes. But this one instead of being different and various colours of brown, grey and golden had pink eyes and light shaggy pink unique fur, and a large, magnificent horn coming off of its head. Its eyes shone majestically.

But to her it didn't look scary, it was just an amazing creature.

She wanted one!

"That. My Hope is a unicorn. That is also a baby one, so we do not want to get to close to it in case mama and papa unicorn arrive, and then they go for us. Which they would trust me, my Hope. They will already see me as a predator when they sense my inner wolf from the off."

"Like the dragons."

"Mmm hmm."

"I kind of like you thought of you as my predator and chasing me as you go." She flirted just a little with the muscled wolf prince.

"Hmm well you are the only female that I would ever dare to chase through the city after." He gave a bit back to her.

"Good. Cos your all mine Clay." She said running a finger down his face. Feeling his stubble, where he needed a shave.

"And you all mine." He growled out. His inner beast was obviously as dominating as its master was.

She hadn't taken Clay as the romantic type on meeting, but he had changed Hope`s mind on discovering that they were destined for each other. He wasn't the hearts and flowers type of guy no, but he showed his love for her in other ways, though he had not actually said it yet! But then, neither had she. It was early days after all.

"Are you sure you want to walk there Hope? For it sounds like we have a long trip ahead of us from where my parents say grand mama has relocated." He said to her, forever concerned for his mate like she was the only female in the world. To others it could be stifling his possessive nature, but to her she found it aptly sweet.

Most of the time anyway.

"Yes, it will be nice. Just the two of us, for a while." She hugged him tightly, smelling his masculine scent and they ended up kissing passionately, and trying not to rip each other's clothes off right there and then, and they had only just left the confinements of the palace!

"Yes, very nice." His eyes twinkled mischievously in joke mockery at his pleasing to him, mate. He knew that she would secretly prefer for them to get a horse and cart, or to try to use the Jetters that she so wanted to try after seeing shifters zipping about on them, but she knew that his wolf preferred his own two, or should it say four feet to get around.

So, she sacrificed her happiness for him even though she needn't to. It did not matter at all though, not really for he would make it up to her in other ways.

She swatted him on one of his humongous, muscled arm. His arms were thick as her thigh, but then he was rather thick all over...

She told him the score.

"Look buster, if you keep groping me and man handing me at every opportunity, then we will never get to your grandmothers before we die of old age!"

"I want to enjoy my pleasing mates beautiful face and teasing wet body though." He drawled, wiggling his eyebrows, then pretending to sulk.

Yes, he would miss his son greatly that he would, but he knew in his heart that his boy was in safe hands in the palace without him, and he wanted to spend some alone time with his new mate, as was usual for new mates.

They had a lot to learn about each other, and he couldn't wait. Patience was not Clay`s strong point.

Ruddy had spent time with aliens being held in imprisonment then time again with his dad when they were reunited, and their new friends from another world.

He needed to be back as a child, back with kids his own age, and learning to control and get used to having a wolf of his own. He was doing well with it so far; he was a great kid that they both knew and were proud of.

He needed this time with Hope, to bond, to make love and to learn.

He also wanted to make her love his planet as much as he did so she wouldn`t ever leave him...

"Clay, we have all the time in the world to do that. I promise you." She said huskily, as they continued walking on with less bags then before, this time.

If he had had this way, he would have put the whole contents of their apartment in their bags!

He stopped at that comment that hit him hard in the chest painfully and faced his one. "Do you though?"

"What do you mean?"

"I mean, what are you going to do when it is time for you to go back to Kalosip, my Bekuna? Will you go back there and make me always alone, or will you stay forever with me?"

"I...I haven`t thought about it." But she had. Over and over.

She pulled his arm to move him forward gently, as they needed to keep going on their path forward rather than keep stopping, for otherwise they would never make it to where they needed to both be.

He turned to her. "Hope, my one. Do not deny it, for I know you have pondered it. I know that is the reason why you often drift off into space for a time. You are thinking serious thoughts, when you do that my female. That you are. It is a hard choice my Hope, me or your home world. But I know what I would pick though..." He smirked confidently with a mask of knowingly when inside he was not so brave at the idea of her leaving him

It would kill him. Literally.

She just laughed at him, unaware of how much the subject eroded his insides.

"We will talk of this another time, ok? Did you bring the map, and the phones?" Which she was still getting the hang of.

"Yes, and yes. And there is no time like the present to talk about it, is there not?" He enquired in a pushy manner.

She was fuming.

"You're not going to let this go are you, Clay?" She snapped at him, pulling back from his grasping reach.

"No."

"You, you!"

Suddenly Hope let out a strange warning growl which shot straight out of her lips, and her eyes shone out bright, like rising suns. They went from brown to yellow, but instead of changing back they just stayed there. Not changing back at all like usual.

And then she spoke but it was not her voice speaking out to him, no, it was someone else`s, from deep inside her.

"I told you to change the subject."

"But I wanna know."

Her eyes rolled back in her head causing him to grab her in shock.

"I said. Stop!" She screamed out in the foreign sounding scratchy but bold voice. She looked like something for a moment had taken over her body. And then she was back.

Clay tried to speak out loud, to apologise to his cross mate, but he found he couldn't talk. He gasped and his eyes grew wide in panic when words did not come out of his thick lips when he tried so. Was he ill?

"Clay, Clay what`s wrong? Say something!" She panicked. She could feel his unease through the mate bond.

And with those words that she spoke, he let out a big sigh of relief and gasped. And then he twigged what had happened. For his dad had done it to him and others before. But...

"You, you. But how?" He just said stumped. He was stunned. He stood tall and folded his arms and looked confused and a bit scared at his mate for answers, that he was not sure she could give him.

"Clay?" She was worried now.

"You gave me an alpha order?"

"I don't understand. What you mean like your dad does?" She tried to joke, but the joke fell flat on its face. "Does that mean I`m the boss of you?" She chuckled.

He didn't smile though. He gritted his teeth instead as though he wanted to say something but chose not to.

He faced her then serious. "It means you gave me an alpha order Hope, and yes like my father does! You told me to stop talking with a strange inner voice, like you have a wolf, but you don't.... And then I tried but I couldn't talk. At all." He pouted.

"What do you mean you couldn't talk?"

"It is what it is Hope. It means I physically couldn't talk. You said not to talk, so I didn't, I couldn`t. It means Hope, that my dad is as long as I have known so, the only planets alpha. But now it means you are... another alpha!

And that was just the start on their journey of shit getting weird.

CHAPTER EIGHT.

"I`m sorry Clay, I didn't mean for that to happen." She hung her head feeling ashamed. She didn't want to be the one to cause her fated mate any kind of upset, not now and not when they had a long road ahead together.

And as they were fated mates, it would kill her if he rejected her like he did Star!

"Its fine." He just said.

But It blatantly wasn't. He was not happy no. Happy, chirpy flirtatious Clay had left the building, and now in his place was a moody sullen male.

She tried to break the ice and get through to her stubborn brooding mate. She didn't like seeing him like this, and felt he was mad at her!

She spoke.

"look I`m not after your job Clay as alpha, if that is what you are worried about. I am still getting my head around being your second when it's the time for you to rule, let alone wanting to steal your future position of the first!"

He scrunched his face in a grimace and scowled feeling shock run through him. Did she really think that?

"Is that what you think?" He glared.

"You said I`m an alpha? I can't help being a bossy bitch, but I am not no alpha."

He seemed sad, as though she had taken his last bar of chocolate, that he was saving for later.

"Look let's just make camp down this long track for the night. A few hours walk down here, and there is the perfect secluded spot for us to lay our heads. I need some sleep Hope, and my head is spinning with every new piece of information that I receive, coming my way."

"Sorry." She dropped her head feeling more and more glum, and they continued walking in never ending silence, until they at last reached the hidden caves where Clay knew they would be safest for the night.

He was a stubborn old fool if he ever was! He decided to set up their sleeping gear in the warm and dry part of the cave where there was less damp and set up traps at the entrance for any predators that might go too close to the other half of his soul.

Hope seemed to keep out of his way since she had accidentally given him the alpha order, and she gave him evils when she thought he wasn't looking her way. But his wolf vision was perfect, and he could see everything, she had obviously forgotten that one!

He got their sleeping bags out of their large back packs, and then left her grouchily pottering around the cave, but also keeping her firmly in his sights, to get them some water for their bottles from a nearby stream. He took more time then was needed and therefore when he got back half an hour later or so, she was fast asleep already!

He could have kicked himself he really could have, what a moron he truly was earlier on! He knew that she wasn't trying to be an alpha and to steal his job. But he just didn`t know why or how she had given him an unintentional alpha command. And his wolf had responded to it. It wasn't because they were mates, no. Something somewhere was amiss, and they needed to put all the pieces of the puzzle together to solve the equation. Before they could solve what was happening, they needed to rest.

Once the bottles of water were stored away for safe keeping, he gently took his sweet sleeping mate lovingly with care into his arms, carefully put a large arm round her so as not to wake her, and he fell into a light sleep beside her.

Enjoying her blissful and sweet scent. For one couldn't be too careful out in the dangers of the open.

But however, when he woke up in the strong morning light, he felt weird like he had been in an extremely deep sleep, instead of the light one he should have had. He felt groggy as anything, like after an all nighter on the Triumph scotch, and his neck pinched rather sharply like it had been pricked with something sharp. It stabbed like glass was embedded in it.

It was weird that he felt pain from whatever it was that had stuck in his neck, as wolves generally healed well and rather quickly, unless it was a major injury that is.

Oh no! He realised looking over at the empty sleeping bag, that his Hope was not beside him where she belonged. But instead of his future queen there beside him were two empty syringes that didn't belong there, with a few mere traces of a liquid left at the bottom of them.

He sniffed them anxious for clues, a feeling of dread hitting him in waves, he sweated profusely with sweat dripping from his face, and then looked around the dark, dry cave with his sharp wolf senses. He sniffed again. He knew that smell that was but from where?

Then it hit him. He had smelt this liquid back at the packs jail a long time ago, when a few rogues had gone nuts and rampaged through the city, and they had had to save themselves and everyone who was there in their path been put into a temporary sleep.

Then if they didn't comply, into a permanent one that is.

It then dawned on him. He had been knocked out! But why? And where on Triumph, was Hope? His Hope! He could cry, and that was rare for an alpha blooded wolf.

His wolf was whining with distress inside.

"Hope, Hope?" He called out and looked around the caves hopefully and in the near outside, in the hope that he was wrong or in some crazy dream world. But with his senses, he could to his despair sense no other person around him. He was all alone with just his sorrow, and also no idea where his mate was, or who had taken her...

And he remembered, it coming back to him now, that he had been so off with her right before she went to sleep for the night. She would have been taken whilst at the same time thinking that he was mad at her! And who would have the nerve and dare to take the princes precious mate? For he knew no matter how mad she felt with him, he was sure that she wouldn`t have just left on her own accord like that!

She would have let him know!

His wolf then before Clay could think any further lost its cool, and shot out of his body in a flash, quicker than it had ever done so before! It didn't give a shit what its master thought. His mate had been taken, he and his wolf were both mad as shit, and they were both out for whoever did it`s blood!

There would be a river of it.

When he found out who had taken her then they had better hope she was safe and well. So that their death was to them, quick and painless for them, rather than him going absolutely berserk, and ripping their head of their shoulders in one quick swoop with his fangs and claws!

His beast howled and howled. The problem was that they had just mated so the bond was new. If it had been further down the road, he could have sensed her, located her from wherever. But as she was wolf less and it was early days, he would have to chase her scent.

The wolf paused. Then it reacted. It started sniffing the ground, tracing her scent, his Bekuna flower that was forever etched in its heart. Good, he had found something! And he left in search of his mate, before it was too late!

For him, and for her.

His inner wolf ran and ran, and it ran. He ran down the long-beaten track, he ran through the curvaceous hills, for miles upon miles, until its paws were sore and bleeding from pounding the ground and hardly resting and knew that he needed to stop at a nearby stream to drink as he was getting dehydrated, and to wash its fur to keep itself cool in the blazing now afternoon sunshine.

He could not stop to find shade as usual, for he had no time to. For every second counted when she was apart from him.

He followed her trail wherever it led, everywhere and anywhere. Enjoying the sweet, familiar scent of her, but missing the smells owner so darn bad that it hurt. But then as he seemed to be finally getting somewhere and possibly reaching some sort of conclusion, the trail ran cold. It just disappeared into thin air...

But how? He should be able to scent her from anywhere. Was it blocked somehow? What could he do now?

Clay quickly changed back from his distressed wolf, into his even more distressed person form, on remembering that he had cut and run from his stuff and hers back at the caves, and so he went begrudgingly back to get their vital things that they needed, and then he carried the bags back on his way.

On his way to find his Hope. His bounded one. For if he didn't, it would haunt him forever...

But then the next thing he knew, to his great surprise came something that he wasn't expecting...

"Clay, Clay? It's me!" What the! Hope`s voice spoke out clearly inside his throbbing, weary head, as if she was right there next to him, by his side as she should be right then. But how? For she had no wolf of her own to mind link to others with, as only wolves could do actually it! He should know he had tried stupidly to link her before! But there had been zilch. Nada.

So how on Triumph, could she speak to him through the pack link now like a wolf who was part of his pack?

Weird. Nothing surprised him anymore. He was just happy to be able to talk to her as the scent had just vanished!

"My Bekuna, are you ok? Where are you?" Who has taken you from me? I will annihilate them all! I will destroy them..." He quickly asked forever raging, his wolf snarled tittering on the edge of destruction. It wanted payback!

It wanted to destroy everyone and everything in its path until it had her back!

Not good.

She explained in a hurried whisper, as though someone might be listening somehow.

"He took me while we slept. I don't know why, I didn't do nothing wrong to upset him, but he took me anyway! And I couldn't do nothing as he injected me with some weird stuff that made me sleep. I just woke up being carried away, he was quiet as so we couldn't have known! ... He doesn`t know we can talk like this.... In the mind." She sounded scared, which did not sit right with Clay. When he....

"Who did? Give me his name!" He roared. His beast wanted answers. And so did he"

"I don't know what his name is! But he`s scary as Clay. And his wolf is blardy mad! He is one of those rogues anyway, I think. Oh god, oh god he`s coming back, I can hear footsteps outside and the key being turned!" She panted anxiously over the link.

He was amazed still, but glad that they could talk this way. For he did not like the idea of her all alone with an anonymous madman, and he could reassure her this way.

For Hope was a strong woman yes, it was one of the things that he loved most about her. But she was still being held prisoner out there by someone. Even the bravest of souls would have found issue with that...

He tried to sooth her.

"Stay calm for me my Triumphian princess, and I will wait for you to get back to me soon, ok my mated one? Remain calm for me, and don't give yourself away to them under any circumstances. I will find you; don't you worry about that. And when I find you, I am never letting you go again."

He sighed full of regrets for before when he overreacted about the alpha command.

"Ok. He`s talking to someone outside with his key in the door. I`m stuck in some room chained up, I can't move far. It's not a modern home, like all the places you've shown me in the city. Like a little cottage back home. Basic."

Clay struggled to stay in control of himself. His wolf nearly went bear-shit crazy on hearing that, its claws coming out of his hands wanting to rip the fucker apart and pull its eyes out! Feeling crazed with its madness at learning that relevant info from her.

Chained up! How fucking dare, they do that to their future one and only queen! Chaining his future Luna and queen up like a mere flea-bitten dog! How dare they touch what was his! She belonged to him! Just him!

He would rip them a new one! He just wished that he could send her his own strength in order for to escape her prison hell hole with ease...

He then after that for a mere moment felt dizzy. As if someone had gone inside him and took most his strength from inside his large statured body. And now he was actually seeing things! He could see Hope reaching for him, reaching into him like he was made of air.

Spooky.

But she wasn't there though...Could things get any worse? He had brought Hope back for a new beginning, a fresh start for them both, but then it seemed that here it was just as much a struggle as back there on her homeland.

He didn't care about being the fucking alpha. It was all he had ever wanted, true. He could not deny it, but he had wanted a family more. And his son, mate, sister and parents were it. His answers to true happiness. He would rather lose his position in the future as alpha then ever lose his family.

He needed to think straight and try not to let her down by doing anything hasty and rash, when what she really needed as her rock was for him to be level-headed now the most. She was on a strange planet, and had been kidnapped, just like he had a few months prior.

He knew how it felt. But then he had his sister and son. Hope had nobody. She was truly alone with a monster!

He ran his thick fingers through his curled dark unruly hair, which was in need of a clean, and tried to concentrate. But all the running for miles in the soaring dripping heat he was still getting reused to being in, had zapped his only remaining energy to the bear minimum, and he was still getting the drug that he had been struck with out of his system.

He stopped briefly and a took a cereal bar out of his bag, and then took a large bite out of it. It was tasteless, he could taste nothing but sorrow and despair. His wolf needed meat, but he did not have the stomach to hunt and eat while she needed him. His wolf would have to wait!

Where was she? She said she was in a room in possibly a cottage, she had informed him, but there was no houses down this way that he knew of for miles...

Most packs liked to keep together and all of his one lived in the city together, so the culprit was obviously not from the city.

Then he had a nasty sudden thought of who could have taken her. A cold unsettling chill ran down himself, at the thought of who it might be. He hoped to Triumph that it wasn't this person, he truly did, because the thought of his one with that monster, didn't bare thinking about...

And he had done them wrong. In their mind anyway.

Because if it was this person then they was unhinged. He knew of a rogue that had taken his residence up in his own turf just out of the city. Clay had gone lenient on the guy when he had gone well and truly mad and tried to start on the main pack, given the circumstances to his wanting to leave the pack.

Orlando.

He already hated the royals with a vengeance and now he would be even more mad due to recent events that had befallen them...

Just then his mind took a sharp turn, as Hope came back into his mind clear as day. He sighed in relief.

"Clay, Clay, I managed to escape! I don't know why, but I got a massive wave of power run through me like it came from you, and I knocked the stupid guy out, then his friends. I think it was from the mate bond, as I thought of you and then I got a major rush, and I saw you right there!"

He smiled for the first time that day.

"Well done, my mate. I am so proud of you, my beauty. Tell me where you are, and what the males name is, who will soon be meeting his death by my claws?"

"Orlando."

He shook his head although she could not see. "I should have known."

"It doesn`t matter Clay, we will talk when we get to each other. I miss you so much."

"Me too. Hope?"

"Yes Clay?" She said.

"I am sorry. I don't care if you rule over me for the rest of my days, I promise you. You rule my heart, my head and my soul anyway, so what is for all of eternity? I just want you back, my Bekuna. With me."

He could hear her sniffing silently. He so badly wanted to have her there in his arms. Just to see her for himself, just to know in person that she was ok. To see it for himself.

She spoke though the mind link again with clarity.

"I`m in Tabrias town, I have just seen a welcome sign for it. I am running but to be honest sweetie, I am blardy knackered!" She sounded it too. He would carry her just to rest her weary feet if he was there with her.

He knew where that was though. She was in a peaceful isolated town, two towns away from the city, where quite a few rogues had gone to hide out. He then to his horror heard something screech loudly in the mind link, and he told her to hide, hide from whatever it was as she gasped in surprise and hide from the crazed wolf, who had snatched her from his arms!

And told her to stay there, for he was coming for her!

Just as he always would.

CHAPTER NINE

He hid their stuff to one stuff behind some tall jagged, dark green bushes, not that many people come out this way and he set off again as quick as, running in his more quicker wolf form. Now he knew where he was heading and who he was after, and where his mate was, then his rapidly beating heart was starting to slow itself down, now he wasn't so anxious about what was happening to his mate.

Suddenly he could feel movement up ahead near a lake. He remained as ever on guard of things and pricked his ears and focused with his eyes. He moved forward slowly, inch by inch and saw what it was. Animals. Hmm mealtime! He slowly but surely approached a pack of deer like creatures his fangs out and fanged mouth now drooling, at the creature that also looked mixed with some kind a bird- Anahondas.

A strange type of animal.

One was flagging behind the others that it was travelling with by a long way, its leg twisted sharply at a tilt in pain as though it had been caught in a trap which it most likely had. It`s beautiful feathery white wings on its back were deformed.

So, his wolf clever as it was, decided to kill two birds with one stone, and put the creature out of his misery.

And he killed it.

It wasn't the tastiest of meats that it had tried no, but the wolf was so hungry for meat that it did not care. Its master had been brooding badly over their stolen mate and had either forgotten or refused to eat anything for some time. But much as his wolf was in a complete and utter worry about their mate also, they both were, it was essential that his master looked after them.

If not, the wolf had decided to take control again until its master learnt his lesson.

For a wolf needed substance to survive, it was an animal after all. Without it, it would be weak and vulnerable like all the other animals roaming free and wild there on the planet Triumph. Well minus the unicorns when on a rampage, and the flying, fire breathing dragons that is. Those fuckers could take care of their self!

Suddenly as he was chomping the creatures fleshy meat with his wolves gaping mouth and enjoying the sour but better than nothing taste of the tender meat. All the Anahondas started running and screeching as though they were being followed and wanted to get away fast. And then to Clays wolf horror, it was grabbed from behind and poked with something sharp in its side.

It howled in pain and dropped the remains.

Then before he could blink, he was thwacked across the head stunning him for a moment. He felt dizzy and like the world was spinning and taking him with it.

He tried to straighten his head, because he was in danger that was for sure. He could see something blue out the corner of its eye, and a tall, wilted shadow. What was it? He could barely move, and his head was sore like it was being crushed in a large vice.

And then his wolf guessed what it was that was hunting him. For an oniony smell lingered through the breeze, it hit his smelling senses full force with a vengeance! The smell made him gag as it reached his taste buds, and bile hit his throat.

No, no way! A smell that he thought he would never smell again as long as he drew breath. It was the smell of a Hazguard being. They nearly all washed, he knew for he had seen it for his self. So, the weird tingly smell, which was just their natural scent. Onions, with a hint of drains thrown in.

Lovely.

He was not getting abducted again, oh no! He couldn't survive it next time, it would be the end of him it truly would, being back held against his will and treated like a slave! And there was no way that he was leaving alone Hope here to the advances of the predator Orlando, while he was taken off into the depths of space by sheer brutal force!

He and his wolf would rather die a painful death then be separated from the other half of it. Last time he did not know that he had a mate, but now he did. He would be of no use as a prisoner for all he and his wolf would do was grief for their mate who was so far away.

No, he must fight!

He could feel the way, like it had happened before, a forced bond being gradually put round his neck and his wolfs energy and magic was slowly leaving at contact with it and its magic depleting abilities, so he decided to transform to make it harder for the bond to be placed around his neck.

The bond that would keep his wolf inside, and unable to be released while it was on. That and the Hazguard`s deadly spiked heavy weapons would stop him in his tracks.

Put the break on things.

Last time he had had the bond on for agonising six months and had nearly gone mad in the process. Forced to do manual labour with little to no break or sleep on a strange cooler planet, and his family threatened by torture and death, if he did not obey the blue, brutal beasts wishes.

He turned round to try to save his skin, and he and the alien struggled against each other. The beast trying to bond him as his prisoner, and he trying to get the fucking thing off of him! The alien looked at him, trying to make eye contact with him, obviously not aware that Clay knew the truth. Clay knew that the aliens could hypnotise you with just one look, eye to eye. He made not to look it in the eye like it was madusa. But whereas turning to stone by looking directly at it he would turn into a slave. A slave to a harsh, vile species of aliens. He would rather die.

He managed to knock it to the ground, its lanky blue body hitting the soil with a thud, and then hit it with its own weapon. It snarled and tried grabbing his arm with sharp claws leaving a large mark.

"Hjsjkdkddkdksparw" it spat out in its own scratchy language.

Clay had no clue what it even meant, but he frankly didn't care at all anyway. For soon it would die horribly by either his hands or his paws, and he would have no need to know its words.

He kicked it in the head hard with a hard thick foot as he tried to get up from the floor where he fell. He had sadly no shoes on to increase the kicks power, as he could only transform form in shorts. The less clothes on turning to your wolf the better, for the shifters!

And then as he fought hard against the blue, gross beast, his firm fists against their lanky ones, the true wonder of the day began. A flash of red came from the cloudless sky above him, and the loud and scary roar of what could only ever be a magnificent dragon hit his ears hard.

The Hazguard tried to get up of the ground to run away from the danger from above, Its black beady eyes wide as they could go in shock at it. But it unlucky for it tripped on its own lanky blue legs as it was injured, and then to Clays up most relief, the dragon pounced the alien who was attacking him, from above.

The dragon threw its weight at the blue ugly one. It had no chance after that!

The alien was then unluckily for it, incinerated. Burnt alive and to a crisp by the dragons flames that poured out of his mouth like a furnace! Clay looked. There was Hope clung to the dragons back, with all her might as so not to slip! It was not something they would relish seeing or hearing, the screams of a on fire alien, its skin and flesh melting like it was a candle.

But it was either the alien met his death or Clay could have been bonded on the neck again, and took away...

"How?" He had no more words but that on seeing his princess. He was speechless, at what he had just witnessed. He didn't care about the alien; he was glad it was dead. Good riddance.

And now his Hope was back! The future was brightening.

"Clay meet Jeffrey. The dragon." Hope beamed from the back of the enormous red scaled dragon that she clung onto for dear life. She bravely patted it gently on the head, as though it just was a pet dog, rather than the big as a house, fire breathing dragon that could burn down cities with its breath.

He shuddered and took a step back from this freakish Jeffrey that was eye balling him like he was a threat to Hope!! It was obviously the same dragon as the one from the castle previously. The dragons all looked unique to each other, not that many got a close look at them up close!

"You have got to be kidding me my Bekuna. Not only did you tame a wild dragon like you were a master, but you managed to not only beat the beast and ride on it as though it was a mere pet. Did you also command it to kill the Hazguard? Are you OK? I was so worried about you, my flower." He beamed.

"I`m fine, my Clay." She said. He was pleased.

He blushed sweetly, a warm glow hitting his dark, handsome, noble face.

"Orlando is still after me though."

She said simply and sighed and hopped off of the large as life fire breathing dragon, who laid down onto the long grass so that she could get off it safely and with ease. And it then to Clays currently on edge relief, it took one look back at Clay and flew away after rubbing its head on his mates arm in a friendly gesture of goodbye.

"Bye Jeffrey safe travels." Hope said waving sweetly. It flew away. Thank goodness.

Clay still felt like he was seeing things and tripping, he truly did. His strong crazy ass mate was as usual full of surprises that he could never so guess what she was going to do next! He would never tire of her or her mysterious ways!

They ran into each other's arms like they were the main characters in a slushy movie, and he held her ever so tight, like he never wanted to let her go.

Which he didn`t.

Inhaling her fruity, flowery mate scent that was radiating off of her, drawing him to her whole essence. The scent that he and his wolf would never forget, or ever grow tired off.

For she was his to keep.

But then the sound of growling came from behind. Hope pulled away from Clay and he pulled her behind him in a protective shield.

There on four paws was a wolf.

But it did not look large and magnificent like Clays wolf. No, it was large, shaggy, grey and it looked mean.

"Orlando." Clay spat. For he recognised the dirty, dark wolf stood before them. The wolf inched closer, uncomfortably until it was at their feet snarling and rapidly blinking as it eyed Clay.

"Face me in your man form! Or are you too much of a wimp to?" Clay said sneering. And standing tall and thick, not showing fear to the wolf who wanted to harm them, but in its wolf form while they weren't. To harm his mate, which he would not allow.

In a flash the wolf turned into a lone male. He was big in size, but not as big as Clay was. The strange male known to others as simply Orlando, paced on the spot in his built-up agitation. He had brown, dirty unkempt hair compared to Clays black hair, and it was straight with no curls, like Clay`s gorgeous ones that covered his head.

He looked in appearances to be of a similar age to Clay, but he was not as pleasant to look at, compared to the bulky prince.

The male looked permanently miserable as though he had had a hard life, which he probably had and had a big sneer on his twisted face. A rough looking scar lay under his left eye, a jagged mark as though he had been stabbed there.

He was wearing shorts with a big rip down them in certain places that thankfully to Hope, still concealed his arse and dick. He had stunk earlier when he took her. He did not obviously have the wealth that the city folk were accustomed to and were used to.

"Oh Clay. Long-time no see." The eerie male said to the shifter prince in a mocking taunt to the prince of all the shifters. His words scratchy like long pointed nails down a chalkboard, as if he didn't often speak a loud, and spent much time alone with his thoughts

"Oh, and if isn`t my lovely looking out-worlder prisoner!" He said taunting yet again, looking at Hope who was peering scared and shaking nervously on seeing her captor again around her mate, at the male who stole her before.

Clay saw red.

He shouted at the male in a dangerous tone. "She is lovely on that I do agree, but she is mine! Mine! She is no one's prisoner, for she belongs to me! For she is my fated mate...." He nearly exploded in his anger at the dirty rogue and his taunting, pushy ways. Clay looked like he could burst a blood vessel!

He frankly knew now that he should have killed the dirty rogue the last time that they met back then, rather than stupidly helping him to flee the city, to get away. He was supposed to be a prince, not a pushover!

Hope who was usually gobby as they come, and generally had no filter that she knew of, decided this time to stay back, for she trusted that Clay would have a handle of the situation.

After all her fated, one was the soon to be alpha king! And he was major pissed!

"So did you tell your lovely mate why I am so angry with you, my prince?" Said Orlando.

"No, she does not need to know, it means nothing." Clay said matter of factly. To him it didn't.

"What doesn`t?" Hope grabbed his thick elbow.

"Oh, shall we begin then? I will relay the story, if the future alpha will not." The rogue sneered.

Clay had eye contact with it at all times, there was no way that he was turning his back on it in case it stabbed him from behind!

"Clay?" Asked Hope.

"It doesn`t matter Hope." He repeated again. His eyes glowed bright yellow, and he let out a small warning growl to the rogue.

Never to his mate.

"Well, it obviously does!" Stated Hope.

"I am, or should I say I was while she was alive, fated mates with Star." Orlando revealed to the now stunned speechless woman.

Hope gasped. She had not expected that. When he had captured her before he had just said over and over, how Clay had done him wrong, but little else.

He continued.

"And she didn't want me no. For she was too busy shagging Clay over here back at the palace!"

Hope glared at Clay through narrow brown eyes, with a hint of yellow to them. "Is this true?" She hissed. She looked so hurt by this news. Clay could skin the male alive for his stirring words!

He drawled in his thick normally irresistible accent. "It wasn't like that my Bekuna." He pleaded.

"Well, what was it like?" She said tearfully. Rubbing the liquid away from her eyes. Yes, Hope was no virgin either on meeting him, or she would not ever pretend to him she was. She was who she was, and she had had lovers too. Both male and female in her twenty-six years.

For she had had no preference to either, she liked the person, the soul, the personality. The sex of the person was irrelevant. But now that she was mated with Clay, there would be no other. Male or female, she had all she wanted.

But she had been honest to him as she always would do. But the thought entering her mind, of her mate with that jealous evil bitch laying her hands all on him, rubbing his large cock, touching each other before she ever did, sent strong shivers of dislike down her spine.

And jealousy.

And he had hid it from her too! If she had a frying pan with her then she would have smacked him hard over the head with it!

He sighed as the rogue laughed to himself like he thought he was funny. Clay scowled at the other male and turning back to his mate he said.

"Me and Charmain had a kind of arrangement, Hope. We were not attracted to each other, we were best friends as I told you, who were matched together due to not finding our true mates. So, when we both still had what would you say, sexual needs, then we decided to each have our own lovers. Mine was Star before she went crazy, hers was a few random women that we both knew of from around the city."

"Woman?" Asked Hope.

"Yes."

"He`s lying!" Exclaimed Orlando, his eyes blazing in anger. He wanted to win this.

"Are you?" She asked her one, confused now. She was not sure, she felt conflicted by the info.

He had truthfully, always been good to her and this apart from the hidden mate thing was the first thing he had kept from her.

He argued his side, for he was not letting a mangy male beat their bond.

"No! I tell you only the truth. She only liked woman Hope, and only a few knew it. We laid together a few times to conceive a child, of that I am eternally grateful for but apart from that we only were best friends. I loved her, and she loved me but not in that other way. Like the way I love you."

"But you didn't tell me that we were mates for a long time!"

"Wow." Muttered Orlando.

"Hope." He pleaded to the woman, looking deep into her soul, who felt she had been wronged unfairly by him. He reached to touch her.

"I am being truthful I promise you. Star was at it with a few different males, we were just casual, I was one of many."

Orlando growled at that.

"She was aware that she would never be my queen, but when you got here, she for some reason went feral. She rejected Orlando out right when he declared they were mates. I felt sorry for him, so I helped him move out of the city, and away from Star." Her man explained cautiously.

"If you was any sort of prince, you would have made her standby my side! Like she was supposed to!" Orlando hissed.

"You cannot force someone to be with you, that I do know." Clay said looking at Hope who avoided eye contact. She instead looked at the floor. Anywhere but at him.

"No but if you had not killed her, then she may have come for me in the end! To be with me like she should have done at the beginning. Instead, I spent a few years alone in a wood cabin."

"No, she went feral."

"Maybe." Hope said thinking aloud to the shifters, "She went feral because she still wanted him, but she wanted you also."

She herself was in to only one person at a time, but who said what others were like? For everyone was uniquely different.

"You think?" Said Orlando hopefully on hearing that. But then realising again as it hit him again that his fated mate was actually dead, and he would never find out if he had meant anything to the wild, carefree warrior at all.

You had to feel sorry for him slightly. Only a teeny bit.

"You will never know, for I am going to kill you!" Hissed a certain angry as anything wolf shifter, as his wolf emerged from his body, but stayed at the surface. They had been here before.

"I challenge thee for the position as alpha!"

"You cannot challenge me, for I am not yet alpha!" Laughed Clay manically at the joker. What a tool!

"Well then, I will kill you, then all your family. Then I will take back the out-worlder for my own. She might not be my mate no, but she can warm my bed up until she gets old and useless and can clean my home..."

He did not get a chance to finish that sentence.

Orlando screamed in terror as the out-of-control wolf alpha prince ran towards him like a maniac, and he knew that this was a fight to the death. And the rogues chances were stacked against him.

Hope just moved out of the way with a sigh. The tiny bit of sympathy she had towards the grief stricken rogue, had disappeared in the blink of an eye. He had gone too far, and now he would pay the price!

The price of his death.

The prince had no weapons, but he did not require them, or would have any need for them.

As two large werewolves started fighting or their cause, teeth gnashing with sharp points, claws ripping, she decided to get out of their way. She could not bear a repeat of watching Star die. That would not do. She walked away and left the two fighting enemies to it. And went in search of some fresh cool water, for the heat was getting to her.

She was of course worried about Clay and his dreadful fight, but he was a prince! Soon to be king, he had the strength of ten rogues and then some put together! The only reason the blue aliens beat him and his men months before, was due to the wolf concealing bonds that they had created, or they would have been toast too!

Orlando gave it his all, Clay would give him that! But his days from the time that he had opened his thin, scowling lips and said what he did about Clays family and mate, meant that instead of the worn looking rogue spending his days in the palace prison for kidnap, meant he would instead be torn limb from limb, by his superior the future alpha.

With a rip as Orlando`s wolf lay on the floor Clays wolf brought its long pointed like daggers claws through the rogues flesh. Blood was pouring out of its stomach from a bite. And it then took a large toothy bite of its leg which bent with a snap at the pressure.

It howled in its pain. The wolves continued to fight each other through blood, sweat and tears, but although Clays wolf became bruised and sore by all the being thrown about on the hard ground after Hope had borrowed some of its energy earlier, it still was much superior in its speed, build and brutal strength.

Orlando managed to get Clay on his back for just a brief time. When Hope entered her mates head.

"I have just gone for some water Clay; I found some nearby? Ok?"

"I am a little busy here my Bekuna." Clay puffed and panted as Orlando`s wolf tried to kill him yet again. He answered in his mind to his mate. "I will come find you soon." He temporarily blocked the link as he wanted no distractions while he sorted this. He decided once all this was done and dusted, and the trip was over that he and Hope deserved a nice holiday somewhere where no drama or anguish lay.

Orlando realised he was temporarily distracted, found the opportunity, and pinned the princes wolf down. He shook him all with thoughts of his mates running through him. And with a sickening crunch he bit down into Orlando`s wolfs neck. Killing it instantly.

Before he could revel in his glory and talk to Hope to let her known that he was ok, he passed out from sheer and utter exhaustion.

"Clay, Clay?" Hope called to him repeatedly through the mind link. She tried reaching into communicate with him, but it was just empty. Oh my god did that mean. Was her mate dead....? She had no wolf in her body, no, but she anyway ran as fast as she could on the two legs she did possess

CHAPTER TEN.

Clay woke up from what felt like a deep foggy sleep, and he felt through the link, and saw with his startling yellow eyes his Hope grunting and bent over in pain. She looked at him wide eyed, now he had finally awoken like a twisted version of sleeping beauty, she ran over with her slim legs and kissed him, to make him fully awaken from his slumber.

The kinda princess, and the wolf shifter prince.

She kissed him so darn hard with all her might and wanting to wrap her arms possessively round him, like she needed him to survive. Which she did.

Everything about the stubborn, handsome male she would simply cherish forever. She wouldn`t take him for granted any more. She thought she had lost him, and he her.

"Your alive!" She yelled happily throwing her lean arms around his thick and very toned torso. She sniffed him as though he was something good to eat.

Which he was...Mmm. He smelt of one of her favourite scents. The smell of the beach back home, the air mixed with a hint of salt and sand. She wondered if they had beaches here. They must do! She hadn`t asked.

"I hope I am!" He tried to laugh back but was throbbing with ache all over his limbs. Soon he hoped his wolf healing would begin to kick in to aid his recovery, as he currently felt like crap. Groan.

It would take him a few more weeks of being back on the planet, for him and his wolf to regain the strength that they were both used to. His wolf had been kept in the dark so long when they were held prisoner that it would take a while to get things going well for them both again.

In the past he would have fought Orlando off in a heartbeat. It had taken him longer this time, but he had still managed it. He had needed taking down! Clay was glad that his beloved had gone off for some fluids rather than witness the horror of Orlando`s death. He knew that she still felt unease about Stars one. Did she think he was a monster? But then he looked at the way she lit up for him.

No. No she didn't.

That was lucky for now the remains of Orlando laid in a twisted torn heap, with flies buzzing round his corpse. Eager for their dinner.

"I thought you were dead!" She said through a flood of tears, ignoring her captors remains that she didn't care for and the bugs feasting on them.

"No way am I leaving you already!" He groaned.

"But why my Bekuna, was you groaning in pain when I opened my eyes?" He stared at her. Awaiting an answer. Would she give him one?

"I wasn't."

"The truth Hope. Now." He insisted.

"Well.... I have been getting those bad pains from before again. They are in my stomach, and legs, well everywhere sweetie if I am honest with you...But don't you worry." She let out a small smile. Fuck she was beautiful!

He faced her with a grim expression. "Why didn't you tell me?" He said his voice raising in pitch. He then forgot all issues with his self when she explained about the pain, and his worries were back to her.

Typical Clay!

"Look its fine, now you are awake can we please carry on our way?"

He looked at her hopeful face. How could he possibly ever deny her anything? She was his princess, his future queen, he would give her the world if he could. And one day he would, as he would rule over everything!

He couldn't wait!

And she to him just had to utter one single word, anything, and he was hers for the taking. It might not be very alpha of him but if she demanded that he dropped his pants and took her right then, then he would obey.

He would please her in every way possible, and make sure she was satisfied before he was. Because wasn't that what mates did? But he wanted to anyway, not because he had to but because he chose to.

He sighed and rubbed his chin with a hand. Brushing past the ever-growing stubble which now resembled a slight beard. "Ok, but if there is any worsening you tell me at once. Yes?" He gave her a fierce warning look.

He couldn't command her, and he would not try but he could just hope that she for once listened to him.

She knew without needing to be told that he would make a fine alpha one day, and king. Better so then his own father who seemed to be trying but looked permanently worn out from the stress of it all.

She also knew that she much as she hated lying to her mate, she would not tell him of any worsening unless she was on the floor unable to move that was. She needed to get to his grandmother. Like yesterday!

"Sure." She nodded sinfully.

He looked at her through eyes like slits as if he could read her truth. They held hands enjoying the skin-to-skin touch of the other and went in search of the water that Hope had come across so earlier. For he badly needed some fluids down him, and they both needed to find food. Now they were back together.

After he awoke, they spent many days travelling together. Only stopping to eat, to drink, to sleep and on a few occasions when Clay became handsy-to fuck. She discovered that she liked them making love by the waters side and fucking hard on top of the mountains. She did put her foot down with him, much as she wanted them to do it as often as possible, they needed to stop as little on their journey as necessary.

She would have his cock in her all day if she could. It felt at home there, in her tight insides.

"We could have called for directions, if you hadn`t left all our stuff and the maps and phones behind near the caves." Hope mumbled quietly under her breath. Clay gave her a side eye glance, pretending that his wolf hearing hadn`t heard her dissing him! They were lost. A bit.

His cheeky mate! She would get a smacked bum by his thick, large hand later! Proper punishment!

Just then his senses felt something up ahead. Someone was out there.

"There`s people ahead!" Hope felt it too! How, he did not know.

Out of the trees a tall male approached them looking at the two with interest. They were all tall here on the planet, so Hope didn't know why she was shocked when she saw he was tall as well, because they all were like it! All the shifters were tall, dark, and meaty, of various sizes and built for strength. Some more than others. Clays father followed by him; were the largest ones she had seen though.

And her mate was the hottest in her opinion.

"Can I ask what you are doing here?" The stranger asked them with a sword to his side, and one hand resting on it in a tight grip. Wearing a strange top and trouser set with bright floral colours, and leather like sandal shoes. Not from the city definitely not, but not quite a rogue like either...

He seemed cautious to protect those he cared for, rather than dangerous.

"Would you dare threaten the shifter prince, and his fated mate?" Clay boomed to the opposing male, in a deep and dangerous voice that was mainly his wolf entering the fold. Clays wolf wasn't as nice or patient as he was.

"Oh, my goodness!" The stranger exclaimed, letting go off his sword and looking now a bit overwhelmed. He was in shit!

"Your highness, I am dreadfully sorry! For I have never had the pleasure of seeing you with my own eyes! And a fated mate? You are truly blessed. And once again please forgive me." He bowed to the prince, over eagerly.

"I will let it pass." Clay warned the slightly shaking male. "For now."

"Clay!" Hope hissed. "Behave will you! He said sorry!"

The stranger laughed quietly.

"A strong female you have my prince. It is what us males need. My Delilah, my picked mate, not fated is the same. I am Fusron. Is there anything I can help you with sir?" He knelled.

Clay shifted around on the spot. "You don't have to do that. Get up! We I confess, are a tiny bit lost Fusron. I am looking for my grandmother. Her name is Bernetta."

"Ah." Said the flower clothed hippy male. "I know her rather well. I will take you to her as soon as. But I must confess that she does not have long left in this world sadly. A few weeks ago, she went from full of energy to on deaths door. Something is keeping her hanging on here with us. Now you are here to see her, I profess whether it may be your impending visit keeping her from entering the next plain, as you know what she is like. A truly magical female. She seemed to be worse today."

"Oh, no." The mates both said together in tandem. Had they come all this way for nothing? His poor grandmother!

"Come." Said Fusron gesturing.

"Come meet the Dalton village, pack. We are a small pack, but we care."

"As you should." Nodded Clay in agreement.

They followed him whilst taking in the scenery as they travelled. It was nice to finally be back somewhere habitable. The village before them, seemed small and basic, shifters were fishing casually and catching food in the woods with various tools or as wolves. But the people seemed happy as could be.

"I like it here." Said Hope feeling mellow and happy. Clay smiled at his one. He had a good feeling about this place too. Whereas the city the palace was in was full of life, here it was a more chilled out place.

Clay hadn`t travelled as much since he was a child, except to visit packs with his father.

"You know when you are king, we don't have to stay in one place?" Hope remarked.

"Hmm." Clay said. She had a point. There was so much of the world to explore out there, and many places that he hadn`t yet been to.

Their guard took them through to the end of the village where some cabins laid in a long row. "This is my home." he said pointing at a nice family looking cabin with a small garden, swings and slides peeping out from behind it, and a welcoming bench out front. A slightly plump female came out of the cabin and waved at them all, many children followed from behind her.

Wow! Hope wondered how they all fit into the home. It was probably like a Tardis inside.

The new female who had appeared smiled at her obvious mate. She smiled at Clay and Hope struggled to hide back a weird growl. Strange! Fushron explained briefly to his mate who they were, and she was so excited to meet royalty!

Her mate took them away.

"This is Bernetta`s house." He pointed next door to a cabin in a corner. "She is probably aware of your presence anyway." He smiled knowingly.

"Hello, hello?" A feeble voice called out as they approached the next cabin, and the male opened the door wide for them.

The cabin was beautifully decorated as though much love and care had been taken into it. Many years had obviously been spent on making the place a home. Clay and Hope both thought that she could have had a loving place in the palace. But it was obviously not what she had wanted. Or was it?

Clay knew his dad was quiet yes, but he had been shady at times. And he and his mate stuck together. Like they should.

"It just me Bernetta." Explained Fushron. "I have some visitors for you, I hope that is ok with you?" He said.

"Yes, I was aware. Bring them to me." The older lady replied. Fushron opened the door to her bedroom, and they peered round. They could see an older now lean female, lined face yes, but pleasant looking still, laying in her bed covers and propped up with many pillows. She was sipping lemonade that she had sneaked some alcohol into and was scowling at a romantic film she was watching on an old fashioned, large tv.

"Blooming males." She muttered a bit too loud under her breath at the tv.

"I know the feeling." Agreed Hope chuckling. "Hi, I am Hope, pleased to meet you." She smiled sweetly at her mates grandmother.

The lady laughed at that.

As she laughed her oval tired eyes, glowed a deep shade of bright orange. Clay then knew that the male who brought them here was definitely right. His grandmother was fading. And fast. Orange eyes was a sign that the wolf grew weak and feeble.

She did not have long left in the world.

"And I am Clay." Said obviously Clay to her, in a polite for him gentlemanly manner. He had never had the pleasure of meeting her before sadly.

"I know." Said his grandmother the retired past queen smugly to them. For she knew everything, and what she didn't know she would find out!

"Fushron, I need to talk to my grandson and his mate."

Hope gasped. Wow she really was all knowledgeable! Fushron looked a bit put out at that, but who was he to argue with an eighty-five-year-old plus female, ex queen?

He shrugged and went off to find his picked mate.

"Be a dear and make me some more lemonade." She said to her two new visitors. "Oh, and fetch me a bottle of vodka grandson. Then take a seat." She gestured to the chairs lined with material, in her room nearby her big spacious bed.

"Are you sure vodka is wise?" Clay said on returning with the over large bottle and noting that it was the strong stuff! Triumphs finest! The cupboard was full of it he had seen on looking, as though she had stockpiled it!

Yes, they might be mighty wolf shifters, but she was blatantly fading fast, and he did not want to send her over the edge with the vodka!

His grandmother looked at him like he was still a wee child.

"Is this what you have to put up with?" She scowled, talking to Hope.

"Yep."

The woman both looked at each other and laughed in solitude.

The lady looked at Clay. "My boy, I am the past queen, so I can by rights do whatever the heck I like!" She smirked her lined face creasing as she did so. "And plus, I am should we say, on the verge of my impending death, so if I want to get shit faced, then leave me to it!"

Clay and Hope looked at her wide eyed for a second, and she let out a loud slightly crazy cackle, which filled the small room of her cabin up with its sound. Her home also contained a cosy lounge, eating area, cramped kitchen, and a stuffy bathroom. She had her own back garden that looked like either she or someone else had lovingly tended it. They guessed that now she kept to the one room.

"But..."

"Clay, leave her be!" Hope argued to her mate. She admired the other woman. What a woman!

She continued on. "Anyway, we have some questions for you, if you don't mind?"

"Not at all." Bernetta replied. "But first, I will tell you about me. It is relevant."

They nodded their heads in agreement. This would be an interesting story to hear. One they needed to hear. For you couldn't learn about the future, without learning of the past.

So, she started her story slowly pausing for breath every now and again. She told them her story, and why she had left the city back then, and not returned to it. Of why she had never met her grandchildren, or little Ruddy. And why her only son, hadn`t been to visit. Ever.

"It all started after my fated mate Alphen, was brutally murdered by a large group of arguing shifters. The rogues got the blame for it as per usual, but I believe them to this day to be innocent, but the council disagreed and your father, Clay, he was on their side. We were a bit laxer back then in those days, and they were not banished from the city, as long as they caused no troubles to us who made and abided by the royal rules. One of my friends was from a rogue family. It made no difference to me. She was a good friend."

"I decided to leave after the death of my mate for it was too painful to stay there at the palace. The rogues were therefore banished without delay, and I stupidly decided to retire, and give the position of alpha to my son and his dominant mate. She was more suited for the role as the leader, he whoever was not. He`s spineless." She shrugged.

This was not the father that Clay knew though. Was it?

"In retaliation there was a fight. Your father, Clay, banned the whole lot of rogues from the planet that he could get hold of anyway a few escaped and the ruling caused more rogues. It wasn't just rogues banned but their family, their friends and anyone who opposed the king and queen. Even the innocents had to go. It was my mate that died I told them we would find the culprit, but they didn't even give me that! As far as I am aware the banished went on to the planet Kalosip to live. Roughly fifty of them."

"Oh, my god." Said Hope gasping. What a monster! She would never look her father-in-law in the same light again. Or the queen…

"We were there though, and we didn't even realise there were other shifters on Hope`s planet!" Said Clay astounded at what he was being told.

Bernetta replied.

"Ah but they were there, but like you were in your time there, they live in the shadows where your father put them. So, in answer to your question, Hope, yes you are the golden one. You are the one from the prophecy. As you and Clay rule over them all, the rogues will return to Triumph if they choose for a fresh start. The rogues on this planet will forgive you when they see the other rogues return back home. You have wolf blood running through you Hope. One of your grandparents was a rogue. They must have mated with a Kalosipian and that is why you have no wolf, and lighter skin then us all here. So therefore, your parents will possibly return to." She shrugged again and adjusted her pillows.

"I knew you were special." Said Clay rubbing his ones arm gently with a hand. At first sight he had known it.

"I can't believe it." Said Hope shaking her head crossly. How could her parents lie to her about her origins? But then they had always been so guarded about everything and had hidden themselves away, she just thought they were introverted people, and in the end as she aged, they grew sadly apart.

"And those poor people." She shook her head at the sadness of it all. They had been done wrong.

Banished off the planet when they had done nothing wrong! Taking the blame for others because they were rogues! It wasn't right.

"Those that did wrong I agree should be punished, but their families, their friends..."

"He made the wrong decision." Stated Clay simply. Because his father had. There was no more to it.

Bernetta added. "Indeed. I felt you starting your journey to me, and then it stopped abruptly."

"I got into a ding dong with a female who wanted Clay, and then it rained for days suddenly." Hope explained.

"It hasn't rained here in days. Was it out of the blue?"

"I don't understand?" Said Hope.

"My son, he has only one power. He used to annoy me as a child, if he did not want to go somewhere he could make it downpour for days. He can change the weather. Control it. There is a point when farmers will ask for some rain from him as you know what this world is like!"

Hope looked pissed, like she wanted to say something but bit her tongue. Clay did not know what to think any more.

It was too much, in too little time!

"When you get back to the city you must take over as alpha and as king, Clay. With Hope by your side as your destined one, then it will bring them all together in unity. If you don't take over, and your father carries on, then I had a dream, a premonition if you like. If he carries on as alpha then there will be a great civil war, rogues versus non- rogues. And it won't be pretty my darlings no; many innocent lives will be lost."

"My sister Shelly said that I had to be king, for the good of the people." Replied the wolf shifter prince. She had known, she must have!

"Shelly and myself communicate through our minds did you know that? Before she must have gone off planet that is. Is she well?"

"Wow, I never knew... Yes, she is on the planet Kalosip, she has fallen in love with a resident there." Clay scowled at mention of the dreaded Shane.

Hope rolled her eyes.

"Good for her!" Said his grandmother. "Yes, the magic runs in our bloodline, though it is very weak in you and your father. It is stronger when younger and in the females."

"Ruddy!" Said Hope suddenly thinking of something. "He knows things too!"

"That doesn`t surprise me." Uttered Bernetta.

"So how come I have magic?" Asked Hope anxiously fiddling with her fingers, looking at the floor instead of their faces.

Did she want to know?

"That I do not know. But your love and return here, will bring the mates to the others. They will dream of their mate and their precise location, and then if they choose to, they can follow that lead. Many will, many will not. The dragons will be allies with the wolves especially as the red one has taken with you, Hope. The rogues will return back home to the planet. And my stubborn thinks he knows it all son, will get what he deserves and be demoted as the alpha."

"You must stay on the planet Hope, forever though I am afraid, to keep the magic alive. If you leave at all, then it will all fall apart!"

Hope gasped. What the! She gulped nervously.

"That is a big ask Hopey, is that what you want?" Clay asked his gorgeous mate, who looked like they wanted to keel over from being overwhelmed.

She looked at him teary eyed. Yes, it was a big ask, if she stayed with him, with his people she could never leave here, ever.... But.... But honesty? She wouldn`t have it any other way. No. For she had, all what she had ever wanted now, a sexy, loving life partner, an adorable stepchild, and a nice place to call home. And hopefully Shane and Shelly, would take up home here too. If they were mates too whether picked or fated.

Clay?"

"Yes, my Bekuna?"

"My home is here with you." She lowered her long-lashed eyes at him. They glowed and his wolves joined in.

And at that gentle reply to the big wolf prince shifter in the room melted deep inside, and he tried not to break down crying. For he had an image to protect.

Future alpha and king.

But those words, were just the best words he had ever heard in his whole existence. His soul sung with merriment, and he felt various emotions running through him, that had only ever happened for him once. When his son first met the world, and when he had the privilege of seeing him for the first time.

She was staying there on the planet with him!

His grandmother grew impatient and rolled her eyes.

"You need to leave. Now. Go home, say I love him to my son, but I regret nothing. And then you darn well take the throne from him! But I have a funny feeling that he will give it to you anyway."

"Will you be, ok?" Said Hope. In the fleeting time that they had met, she had grown fond of her future grandmother in-law. She wished with her beyond caring nature that it was not the way it had to be, and that she could come with them.

But she was too frail, and her home was now here. She reached over and gave her a quick hug on the spacious bed where she lay sipping her lemonade and vodka, cloudy eyed from a bit too much.

"Enjoy your vodka." Hope whispered in her ear.

And with that goodbye, the grandmother smiled, a broad beaming smile. And then in front of their stunned eyes, magic began leaving her soul and coming out of her body for all the room to see, and it went into Clay and Hope who were standing there side by side clutching hands as one. Her eyes turned bright yellow then orange, and she let out a growl then a weird yip, claws came through her hands.

Before they could utter the words that were what was happening? Bernetta took one last long breath from the planets air, returned to her usual form her claws retracting, and then she sadly died.

CHAPTER ELEVEN- THE FINAL CHAPTER

And they left. They went and sadly told Fushron what had happened. He was gutted they all were, and he promised he would send news to the city when he had sorted Bernetta`s funeral arrangements out. He was given a direct line to the palace, which hopefully would be run by Clay by the time of the funeral! It made sense for Fushron to do it. He and his mate had done more for her then her own family had ever done.

Clay felt guilty as anything. But it wasn't his fault.

The whole village transformed in sorrow and howled together on learning of what they called witch wolfs passing. Clay joined them in unity. Their wolves ran together through the small village, in honour of the great elder Bernetta, who had hung on to meet her grandson for the first time, and also the last. But now her magic ran through them both, then they would be able to know things, just like she had.

And they would carry the burden- together.

Clay helped the males of the village to dispose of his grandmothers body, and to put it somewhere to preserve it for a time that it was needed for burial.

"Can we stay the night?" Hope asked Fushon quietly her head hung low. He nodded. There was a spare room for them, so they did not have to lay where Bernetta had just taken her final breath in the world. They both decided that it would be nice to have a roof over their heads for a lone night. They showered which they so badly needed and freshened up, and while Clay relaxed in the garden with his whirling round his head thoughts. Hope pottered silently around the gorgeous cabin. Tidying things up for the late Bernetta and having a nose for clues.

In the morning after grieving solemnly in each other's company, they said goodbye to Fushron and his millions of kids, and had a light walk through the peaceful village one last time. They were not sad no longer, for she would have been happy there it was plain to see. For it was truly a remarkable place to live.

It had more personality then the city ever had.

"Are you ok?" Hope asked Clay sadly coming into the garden, to be by his side in comfort. She had never seen anyone die from old age before, and that, and the out of this world magic, leaving his poor grandmother and entering them without consent had truly startled her!

But she felt blessed. That his grandmother had trusted them to be left with her magic, and that when Hope went to pass, she hoped she would have someone she trusted to pass it on to also.

He raised his head to look at her as she came near. His one. He didn't have to hear her or see her he could sense her with every fibre in his being, his soul.

He shook his head. For he wasn`t ok right then.

"I will be fine in time my love. But I did not know where she was, maybe I should have pressed mother and father a bit harder to find her?"

"Can I tell you, my opinion?" She asked him warily and unsure. He might not like it.

"Any day, my one."

"I believe they did not want you to see her, as we would then hear her truths. What did they say when you said we were coming here after the dragon appearing event?"

"Nothing much, it just kept getting postponed all the time. Then Star came out and went mad, then it rained."

"You don't think?"

Hmm. Had Star been told about their departure by someone`s loose lips? But then something rather strange happened. She could see what had happened back then, she could see it as clear as day in her mind, as though it was there on tape. The magic in her soul from Bernetta's was kicking in, and fast and flowing free through her.

She could see the king letting slip to Star that they were leaving on their journey. Hinting that Clay might be unsure. Then the kings horror at the females death due to his unashamed stirring. And then the heavy rain fall which only stopped when his mate worked out what he was doing. Then back, back to before, when the king saw the death of his father at the hands of a group of shifters. But then he let the rogues take the blame for it, to be rid of them, and their issues. Other questionable things, that as alpha and king he should not have done. Letting innocents take the fall for things and letting those guilty for crimes off.

Realising that Hope was more than likely one of the fallen rogues children or grandchildren and trying to mess up things between her and him by putting doubts in Clays then fragile mind. He loved his two children, his mate, and of course his people you could see that, she knew that, but the king had also done a lot that others were not aware of for his own selfish gains.

Hope looked next to her at her dashing beau, Clay was just coming out of a trance too. He shook his head dumbstruck and gazed at her frowning.

"Did you?" She asked.

"I did." He sighed. "I saw everything. Things I needed to see, and things I had no place in even knowing." He drawled huskily. "I think we will take it to my father, the evidence. And then if he does not back down, then we can threaten to tell the court everything."

"I agree." She said.

And together they left the village carrying only some food, water and other bits and bobs that Fushron had insisted that they take with them on their trip home. He had been fretting like anything, at them both leaving for the wilderness again.

For danger could be lurking without you even knowing it as they all to knew.

The journey home went without any major issues. They did what they had done on the way there. Talking, tasting, and exploring each other, play fighting... And just making the most of each other, before the busy ways of the city that awaited them soon.

That was until the last few days that is after they had camped out in the mountains when they were shortly home....

It had been ok on awakening, but now poor Hope writhed around in agony on the floor of the forest of the camp that they had set up earlier sweating profusely, Clay held her hand sweetly acting and cupped her face worriedly in a tight and protective firm grip and he lovingly wiped the sweat away from her worried face with a damp cloth. He had made it moist for her, from the flowing river nearby them.

She was burning up and nothing could break her fever that he had tried.

Her golden-brown skin the succulent colour of caramel, was beginning to glow on and off in a rather strange way, which looked unnaturally freakish with its eerie shine.

She didn't know what on earth was happening to her or why so? She wondered again why oh why, had she made the stupid mistake to come to this planet with Clay for a time? She was scolding herself now that she should have taken her time and not gone and made such a rash decision to go to there with him. And that maybe, just maybe she should have stayed behind on hers with the safety of her own people.

And those that were like her.

Her bones felt like they were snapping at all angles, and her joints burnt like a raging fire was running itself through them, and she felt like she was being burnt alive from the inside out.

"Clay what is going on here?" Hope said to her handsome companion on their trip for answers, with tears glistening in her usually brown eyes, which disturbingly to look at now had changed to a bright and vivid shining gold yellow, which reminded him of two blazing hot suns during sunrise. They were going from their usual shade of startling brown to a vivid bright yellow, and back again, with increasing consistency like they couldn't make their mind up what shade they wanted to actually so be!

But she looked simply beautiful to him either way, no matter what she looked like. She could wear rags and he would be on his knees begging for her to be his girl.

Clay the wolf shifter prince sighed quietly in his hidden anguish at her obvious excruciating pain, that he so desperately wished more than anything else in the world, that he could take away from her weary body. And put it Into his own one. He would do anything for her, but he feared this was one thing that he couldn't overcome for her.

He turned to face Hope looking rather guilty like a young boy caught nicking sweets from a sweetshop and feeling it beyond anything also.

He didn't know how to say it.

"I think I know what is happening here. But I am not entirely sure of it." He uttered.

But if it was what he thought, then it shouldn`t even be happening at all to her. It couldn't be! Not to his precious fated mate, she was nothing but a good person as ever. She didn't deserve this whole entire, painful transformation that he suspected was happening to her right before his very eyes, and which would be therefore permanent, and keep her from ever returning to her own world.

She begged him, her long eye lashed eyes looking into his own. Her gaze pinned him to his like she was a magnet.

"Tell me Clay. Please. I need to know. I need to know what is happening to me." She insisted that he tell her, no she begged of it. She didn't like the not knowing what was going on right now, even if the answer she got was one that she didn't want to hear right now.

He decided to just say it. "I think your.... I think your maybe turning into a wolf like me, sweetheart."

Like him. But no, not the same as. For if it was true what was transpiring, for not a black wolf like him she would be. No.

But a golden one. The first of its kind ever to be in existence on his planet, and also the last one.

"What!" What the heck! She looked at him both scared and also extremely horrified in one sweep. This couldn't be happening to her, it just couldn`t....

So, she decided to stay in denial, the best place to be right now.

She tilted her aching neck. "I`m not getting a wolf, your wrong that`s stupid! I think I`m dying Clay. That must be it. This must be the end, I can't bare it, I really can`t it hurts so bad." She sobbed openly and screamed out loudly her yell piercing through the land, as a sharp pain like nothing else, ran through her abdomen like she was being repeatedly stabbed in the stomach with a set of sharp knives.

"Or maybe I`m having a surprise baby?" She said as another cramp like what she knew of a contraction hit her stomach. She didn't think that she was able to carry a child, but theses thing could be wrong, couldn't they?

Clay openly growled out at that awful thought. The thought of her carrying a child that wasn't even his, and she looked up tear stricken and frowned at his reaction as she didn't know the extent of his feelings for her right at that moment, and why he growled out loud like he was beyond mad.

She argued with herself.

"But I haven`t you know...haven`t done the deed in ages except with you of recent. It has been more than nine months since another has gone down there so.... Argh! What is this hell coming over me? What have I done to deserve this fresh hell?" She gasped in pain. It was awful!

She did not realise that her words were making the ever in control wolf want to unleash its anger to the world! He did not relish the thought that she had taken another man`s cock before his, even though he had no rights to her back before and he knew she was no virgin.

She didn't frankly care or wonder now why Clay was growing increasingly more agitated, and struggling to reign his beast in. She was into much pain to care.

But as it turned out though, Clay was sadly right. She was actually becoming a wolf. Right then. Right now.

For as soon as she started accepting and believing that it was happening it and rather than denying it, golden brown fur started breaking out over her golden skinned, toned arms, and her teeth seemed to be growing suddenly longer, and extremely sharpened like fangs.

She disturbingly to her horror let out an inhuman growl from her throat and gasped in surprise at the unfamiliar sound being released from her own mouth. She howled, she actually howled!

"I`m.... I`m turning into a wolf!" This was not happening to her, she thought before she passed out from the pain.

And then she did her wolf unleashed through her skin. Clay had never seen anything so horrifying as his mate unconscious and at the same time turning into a wolf.

A light, golden wolf. She was like nothing he had ever seen before with his eyes, or like he ever would do so. But then his mate laying in tears on the ground doubled over was a stunning female anyway in her own right, he loved everything about his adorable, cute one... Of course, if she ever had a wolf, not that they had ever expected she would, then it would be as beautiful as she was.

She was a lean wolf, leaner then a Triumphian wolf. He stroked her golden glowing fur gently with his hands, cherishing the fear of her smooth fur in his thick hands. His wolf eyes glowed yellow, his wolf inside him was so happy that his wolf had a mate for him to run with on all fours!

And then with that he put his stuff back in the rucksack, he packed up their things and then he put his tired mate in her new temporary wolf form, in his arms and he ran with her with his thick legs.

For an entire day he didn't care, he ran with her protectively in his loving hold, until he reached the city now there in his sights. Then he placed his one down carefully and turned into his wolf and he lay with his golden wolfed mate, and he fell into a deep and tired sleep next to her. He snuggled closer to his mate. His fated one. He hoped that soon all his people would be able to like it was spoke of, get the chance to meet their own fated one. Because he was so darn lucky!

They lay curled up together as though they were one. Just as they always would be.

The End.

EPILOGUE

It had taken a lot of getting used to, Hope having her own inner wolf, and being able to transform in the blink of an eye from her usual tall and toned, golden skinned female figure, to that of a brown golden furred wolf beast. And back again if she so chose to do so. Whenever she wanted.

And she could communicate with it! She said to Clay it was like being divided into two and sharing her body with someone else. When Hope was in her body the wolf was inside her, there on the surface but hidden. And when her glorious wolf came out to play, Hope was there but she let the beast take control for a time.

That day back then when she had rested there in her new golden wolf form, collapsed with the pain of it all in Clay`s paws. Two wolves, fated ones at that, at peace with each other's presence, and getting to know one another for a start. It took a while yes it did, for the creatures buried inside them to connect, and to get used to each other's various wild wolf ways. Just like it had taken herself and Clay a brief while too.

When Hope had awakened, she was stunned to learn that she had become a wolf shifter like her fated mate. But there was also a part of her that had been excited that she could become more a part of this world. A world full of wolf shifters, where she had been for a time the only non-shifter person on the whole planet. Now she wasn't!

When she and Clay transformed back to mere people, with him trying to clumsily demonstrate to his oh so precious one, how to transform in her underwear, as she had ripped it all to shreds when she had first transformed! It took her a while to figure it all out, but she`s getting there!

When the two eventually returned to the city, they were met by little Ruddy standing there his hands on his hips impatiently next to the drawbridge of the palace. He threw his scrawny, needing more meat on the bone arms around them, in his complete and utter joy at seeing them. They returned the hug, Hope reaching in and sniffing in his scent, and now realising that her wolf powers had kicked in, and she could now sense his wolf hidden inner too. She could also mind link him. Crazy!

He spoke quietly in merely a hush, on their return to them, so that no one could overhear what the young shifter had to say. The place was strangely empty back at the palace they had noticed it straight away, and even Clay`s parents were not in sight of them or waiting there with welcoming arms.

"I told them that you knew, and that you were coming for them, to take over as the new alpha and his Luna." Ruddy said to them innocently.

Wow, that kid of Clay`s, never failed to amaze them with what he knew. He definitely had magic running through his veins!

They had walked over the long wooden drawbridge, and then had entered the palace grounds. The place was what they could see as empty, except for a few man servants loitering around and staring at Hope, as they smelt that she now had a wolf! They gawped in disbelief!

Clay let out a protective growl and they had backed off! He could be simply put terrifying!

One approached them, the two tired mates standing together as one, and had told them discretely although there was no one that they could see or sense there to overhear, that Clay`s parents were waiting for them in the vast meeting room at the back of the palace near the library, that Hope had seen when Clay had shown her around during her first moments there.

They arrived at the meeting room, hushed whispers behind the door. And they cautiously opened it. Not knowing whether his parents would be happy to see them, or on their guard and arguing for the position as king and his queen.

When they opened the door there, they were. The current rulers of the whole planet there in the flesh. His mother and father. They had wondered whether it would be a peaceful exchange.

They were both relieved when his parents came over and greeted them with nothing but firm loving hugs. Almost like goodbyes, if you read the silent message behind them. There was a lawyer there and everything, and all the council members sat round a large, oval table waiting patiently.

Like sardines in a tin, the room was full of people, much like when Hope had arrived cramped in a small spaceship, with the man who was now her one and only.

The king and queen had pulled away. The king had stood awkwardly, not his usual strong presence and his mate held back to let him speak, for a change.

The king spoke. "I only did what I thought was right at the time." Speaking from the heart with tears in his eyes. Gulping and trying to hold back his emotions but failing miserably. In his eyes he had tried to be a good king, but he knew that he had cut corners where they didn't need to be cut!

"I know." Said Clay simply.

The queen shook gently next to her husband. She had had no involvement in his untoward decisions no, but she had been fully aware of most of them. In Hope`s eyes who turned her head to look at her, that made her just as bad as he was.

The king spoke again. "I have signed over the palace to you. You my son, are the new alpha, and the new king. It is now yours."

"Hmm." one of the more senior appearing council members had said, a senior male with a big dark moustache. said standing up out of his leather backed chair. "It was either that, or you were sentenced for crimes against your people. You have done enough to be sentenced to life or even executed...."

The king had sighed at that and shook his head. "I didn't mean to..."

"But you did." Clay had said. "You did, that is all that matters. You father had a choice every step of the way and you chose wrong on many occasions. Look I care deeply for you both, I don't want things to be awkward between us, I want things to be the same as they were, you don't have to leave here at all." He looked at his parents.

Hope nodded. She tried to let my mate take over.

"And Hope, she will be the joint alpha with me. No alpha and Luna bullshit, she is the golden one, the golden wolf, we rule side by side." He said.

Everyone gasped. Then they all sniffed, their noses high in the air and their eyes all bulged on smelling the new golden wolf deep within her.

She growled dominantly to show them who she now was!

"Congrats dear! His mother said to her sincerely. "And I knew it from the start! We are all saved now!" And she was honestly happy. They all knew that the two had had enough of ruling over everyone.

And now their time ruling had come to early end.

"Thank you, your majesty." Hope had replied to her eyes now a shade of pale yellow and brown never more. "Hopefully now, all will be able to meet their fated mates. It is what I desire. I hope it is true."

The room went quiet.

It was excellent news, for sure it was. But what of those that had chosen another mate, when they hadn`t found their fated one? One of the male council members in the room lightly touched arms with another male. They were picked mates. What would it mean for them both now? Would another male swoop in and take what was theirs?

Would the great thing that was soon coming the shifters way, also be a bad thing to others?

They had hoped not.

There were murmurs sounding, and then the room hushed as the retiring queen had spoken. She was leaving her position gracefully.

"Oh, no." She shook her head sadly. "You, my dear are the queen now!"

Hope had never been more shocked in my entire life! Well, she had known that it would happen, of course she had. As it had gone round and round in her head for days, that soon she would be proper royalty!

The council members offered the Hope and Clay their congratulations. And they meant it. They had been pleased for them, truly.

The new queen just stood blushing while Clay thanked everyone for all they had done. The old king and queen had decided they said, to leave the palace, and Clay offered them the home he had built lovingly with his own hands.

For he did not need it now and it would be a shame to remain empty any longer. And his parents wanted a fresh start. Nearby but not at the palace. It wouldn`t be right.

"We would be honoured!" His mother had said.

Hope had then coughed politely to get everyone`s attention.

"So, this means that the shifters now currently on the planet of Kalosip, and their families, and anyone else sent their wrongly can return." Hope simply stated. It wasn't a question, for it would happen, whether they liked it or not. Those shifters who had left had to be given the choice what to do.

It was their right. They deserved but that.

"Send word to Kalosip." the king said nodding. For he knew when he was beaten!

A council member had quickly gone to find those who could get a spaceship, or three on its way and quickly!

Hope whispered something to Clay, and they had to let the king know that sadly his mother had died. He had been full of grief, but then pleased that his son, and his fated one now had her magic. It would help them on their path.

"We are blessed." Said Clay nodding. "But if we need any rain, or there is a draught then I know where to come!" He smirked at his father knowingly. His dad looked shocked then burst into laughter. He patted his sons arm gently.

"I will do son, I will do!"

The pair decided amongst themselves that the king and queen would have a month to help them, to help them find their feet there before they retired.

And help them they so did.

<u>A month later</u>

Clay and Hope lay in bed together curled up smiling soppy at each other. Whispering sweet nothings in the others ears.

Tired, no thanks to Clay and his over eager banging that night. Filling Hope up as many times as he could.

They had got married the day before. Just them, Ruddy and his parents. Plus, two more. Oh, and of course the vicar! With drinks and a party till late after.

But there was no time for them to enjoy any sort of honeymoon yet no! For today, they were being crowned. King and his queen, alpha and his alpha not Luna.

Nervous butterflies ran up them both, from the inside. But they knew that it would be ok for them in the end. For they had each other, they had their families, new friends, and most of all -the peoples respect. And the shifters from Kalosip were hopefully arriving tomorrow.

They both showered, dressed and got ready for what now awaited them.

Then the door went.

"Hello?" Hope called out. "Come in!"

The door slowly opened and there was whispering behind the door. And there barged in was Shelly and Shane clutching hands and looking at each other in a soppy manner, and Ruddy was there lagging behind them looking a bit traumatised for some reason.

"I`ve had enough of them keep kissing and hugging. It Is gross." Ruddy murmured. Shelly blushed, Shane smirked his blonde curtains falling in waves. and then they all laughed. Clay didn't for once send the other male a stinky look, and for that Hope was proud of him.

If Hope had thought that she had stood out when she had first arrived on the planet, then Shane and his pale skin, freckles, and blonde surfer boy hair, really stood out on the planet Triumph!

"Well, you have come to the wrong place then." Hope said squeezing Clay tight, and them gazing at each other all lovey dovey as per usual.

"Whys that?" Ruddy asked her warily.

"Because I`m going to give you a big kiss!" And he giggled as his new stepmother who he adored so very much, chased him around the room. No, she could not have no child of her own, but this little boy here right now, she would give him all the love in the world. She finally caught him and gave him a big kiss on his head which he quickly wiped off!

Shelly and Shane hadn`t been on Kalosip when word had been sent there that the rogues and their families were free to return. It turned out, that they had been on the planet Hazguard, fighting off evil!

The door went again! Hope wondered how many more people could fit in this apartment! And they were trying to get ready!

Kellon. A shy and sweet female who had been hired to assist Hope, was stood there with a small, handpicked bunch of beautiful lilac-coloured flowers in her hands. She was only twenty bless her and looked so nervous standing there fiddling with her hands.

"Hi Kellon. We did not need you today, did you not get the message sweetie?" Hope said kindly whilst looking at Clay with a frown.

"Oh, I did. I am sorry to intrude. I just wanted to give you these." She handed Hope the gorgeous smelling flowers.

"Thank you these are beautiful." She smiled.

"I shall go now I see you are getting ready for the coronation. Good luck. I just brought these to say thank you."

"For what?"

"I dreamt of my mate last night! I know his name, and where he is. I am so excited" She grinned happily. "It is in the next village, so when I get some time off next, I am going to find him. His name is Lance." She beamed, her wolf eyes shining brightly through.

Hope stood wide eyed. Wow! She shook her head. She was the golden one, so what did she expect?

"It's happening already, my Bekuna. Thanks to you!" Clay said putting an arm around her proudly, as ever her rock.

Hope snapped out of it and asked the girl.

"When are you next due in?"

"Tomorrow, your future majesty." She bowed to Hope.

"I do not expect to see you for a week. Celebrate our coronation with us today, and then tomorrow find him. And say hi from me." She smiled.

"Thank you so much." The girl said, tears glistening in her made-up eyes.

"Your welcome!"

And then she carried on getting ready.

That very day they were crowned king Clay, and queen Hope. The new wolf shifter rulers of them all. The new alphas also. The red dragon came to watch them be crowned from a distance, and they and the dragons came to the city every now and again but generally kept out of the shifters way but causing no more trouble again.

The same day all over the planet many, many shifters dreamt of their fated mate. Some chose to follow that path whilst others decided to stay on the path that they were currently on. Later that day with the new king and queen who had decided to do some travelling, get to know there people. Some of the Kalosip rogues returned, but sadly Hope`s parents were not with them. She was disappointed - yes, yes, she was, but she hoped that one day they would meet again.

The two royals lived for many happy years reigning together as one, and when they passed away at the same time on the same day together as always, their magic passed to Ruddy, where he became the strongest wolf of them all.

Don't miss out!

Visit the website below and you can sign up to receive emails whenever Tanya Coleby publishes a new book. There's no charge and no obligation.

https://books2read.com/r/B-A-FMUS-YNMFC

Connecting independent readers to independent writers.